THE BETRAYAL

by

Jonas Saul

PUBLISHED BY:
Imagine Press Inc.
Ebook ISBN: 978-1-927404-51-5
Paperback ISBN: 978-1-998047-46-8
Hardcover ISBN: 978-1-998047-47-5

The Betrayal
Copyright © 2018 by Jonas Saul

All rights reserved. No part of this publication may be reproduced, stored in a retrieval system, or transmitted in any form or by any means (electronic, mechanical, photocopying, recording, or otherwise) without the publisher's prior written permission.

This is a work of fiction. The characters, organizations, and events portrayed in this novel are either products of the author's imagination or are used fictitiously. References to real people, events, establishments, organizations, or locations are intended only to provide a sense of authenticity and are used fictitiously. Any resemblance to actual events, places, organizations, or persons, living or dead, is entirely coincidental.

Imagine Press Inc. does not have control over, or any responsibility for, any author or third-party websites referred to in or on this book.

The Sarah Roberts Series

Dark Visions (One)
The Warning (Two)
The Crypt (Three)
The Hostage (Four)
The Victim (Five)
The Enigma (Six)
The Vigilante (Seven)
The Rogue (Eight)
Killing Sarah (Nine)
The Antagonist (Ten)
The Redeemed (Eleven)
The Haunted (Twelve)
The Unlucky (Thirteen)
The Abandoned (Fourteen)
The Cartel (Fifteen)
Losing Sarah (Sixteen)
The Pact (Seventeen)
The Terror (Eighteen)
The Chase (Nineteen)
The Betrayal (Twenty)
Sarah's Return (Twenty-One)
The Hunt (Twenty-Two)
The Delivery (Twenty-Three)
The Trap (Twenty-Four)
The Ultimatum (Twenty-Five)
The Depraved (Twenty-Six)
The Condemned (Twenty-Seven)
Payback (Twenty-Eight)
The Unknown (Twenty-Nine)
Wrath (Thirty)
The Damned (Thirty-One)

The Game (Thirty-Two)
The Decoy (Thirty-Three)
The Disappearance (Thirty-Four)
The Whole Truth (Thirty-Five)
Alex (Thirty-Six)
Parkman (Thirty-Seven)
Darwin (Thirty-Eight)
Aaron (Thirty-Nine)
Remains To Be Seen (Forty)

The Jake Wood Novels

The Immortal Gene (Book One)
The Immortal Target (Book Two)

Standalone Novels

'Til Death Do Us Part
The Drowning
The Woman in the Woods
The Threat
The Specter
The Mafia Trilogy
A Murder in Time
Frequency of the Dead

Co-Authored Novels

Collision Course (Written with Gary Ponzo)
There Will Be Blood (Written with Rania Stone)
The Soulless (Written with Rania Stone)

Short Story Collections

Twisted Fate (Tales of Horror)
Twists of Fate (Tales of Hope)

Chapter 1

SARAH ROBERTS WAS TEMPTED to ignore the feeling in her gut as the highway stretched out ahead, heat shimmering off its surface. She fought to ignore that nagging need to ask Aaron to pull over to save lives.

The number of dead resonated in her head. She fished a pen out of the glove box of the rental and wrote down the number on a gas receipt: thirteen dead.

"You okay?" Aaron Stevens asked, snatching glances at her. "You seem fidgety, upset."

She shook her head as images and disjointed messages filtered into her consciousness. The importance was all too real. Duty bound by the knowledge given her, Sarah turned and glared at her boyfriend.

"Pull over."

"What—"

"Pull over!"

Aaron jerked the car to the right and steered onto the wide shoulder of Highway 401. They had buried two friends earlier in the day in Toronto. The funeral over, a visit to the hospital where another friend recuperated after an exhausting ordeal with the Toronto mafia, then a police escort home to change and pack their bags.

All this came after Sarah announced her retirement as a psychic vigilante.

The moment the rental was parked, Sarah hopped out. She walked over and leaned against a signpost warning of deer crossing, a hand on her stomach. Aaron followed close behind.

"Sarah?" He spoke loud enough to be heard over the sound of traffic racing by. "What's going on?"

She gave him the gas receipt.

"What's this?" he asked. "Thirteen dead?" He handed the paper back. "Where?"

"Here." She met his gaze. "It'll happen within ten minutes."

Aaron looked up and down the highway. "Here? As in, right here at this exact spot?" He gestured at the ground.

She shook her head and pointed up the highway. "About half a kilometer away."

"What can we do to stop it?"

Good for him, she thought. No complaints about this being their vacation. No issue with the call to action. Just straight up, ready to get to work.

Her sister's voice echoed in her head. The sister she lost

so many years ago, whispering messages from the other side. Messages of future events, trouble, and death.

Such a morbid sister.

"I can't take it anymore," Sarah whispered to herself. "Are you listening, Vivian? I've just lost two of my best friends. No more." Vivian's voice resonated through her consciousness, and Sarah soon understood it wasn't about her. It wasn't about those thirteen people. This time, it was about survival.

And a vile betrayal.

"Why?" Sarah asked, her voice taking on a weakness previously not heard. "There's a threshold, you know, a point of no return. There's only so much I can take."

"Sarah?" Aaron's voice was tentative, as if he was afraid to interrupt. "Are you still talking to Vivian?"

She wiped away a tear. "I'm talking to whoever will listen. Vivian, God, you, the Universe."

But it was no longer a choice. That comfort had been taken from her. She had to stay and fight. The betrayal would kill her and many others if she didn't stay on.

Vacation soon, Vivian whispered. *You can't avoid this.*

"What's she saying?" Aaron asked, agitated as he watched the highway, the passing motorists, a hand clutching his hair.

"I can't avoid this." Sarah threw up her hands in despair. "Whatever this is." Collecting herself, the old Sarah back, she stood straighter and glanced along the highway, slipping the gas receipt into her pocket.

"She isn't telling you more?" He gawked at her. Their eyes met. She shook her head. "Shit." He slapped his leg. "I thought we were done with this for a while."

There's the complaint.

"Me too." Sarah pushed off the signpost and walked to the shoulder of the highway. The swoosh of wind as a van passed buffeted her hair upward. She held her ground, watching the traffic as it approached. Toronto was back that way. They had been heading toward Ottawa for a much-needed vacation. Time off after too many deaths, too many injuries, and close calls.

Aaron came to stand beside her. "What're we waiting for?" he asked after a break in traffic.

"Not sure."

"You got anything more?"

"Just that thirteen people will die in a matter of minutes."

"And?"

She glanced up at him. "And I have to find a way to stop it."

They stared at each other a moment longer, and then Sarah turned back to the highway. Two large trucks carrying what looked like bridge parts were escorted along the highway by small pickup trucks with flashing yellow lights. They appeared to be going twenty to thirty kilometers below the posted limit. As they approached, Sarah ran back to the passenger seat of the rental to grab her sunglasses.

When she stepped up beside Aaron again, traffic had slowed behind the large vehicles and their cargo. A blue school bus approached in the slow lane, its turn signal on, waiting for a chance to pass. The trucks with bridge parts were already safely by. She watched every vehicle closely, waiting for a signal from Vivian.

Nothing came.

"Could your sister be wrong here?" Aaron asked. "Shouldn't we just get back in the car and move on? Forget the whole thing?"

Sarah stared at the school bus as it got closer. Why blue? Why not yellow?

Her abdomen clenched. She doubled over, a hand on her stomach, a moan escaping her lips.

The blue bus.

A prison bus.

Inmates on board.

All dead, Vivian whispered.

Sarah gasped.

She yanked off her sunglasses and stared at the bus as it moved into the fast lane and came alongside them. A man near the back of the bus stared back at her. He had a look of abject terror pasted on his wet face, eyes bulging, mouth agape. Something told her he knew his life was over—she was certain of it. The man started yelling, his mouth opening and closing like a fish attempting to throw a hook, but Sarah couldn't hear him on the shoulder of the highway. He jumped from his seat, pressed his cheek against the window, and shouted something over and over in Sarah's direction, pointing at her until the bus was lost from sight.

"The bus," Sarah tried to yell, but the sound of the passing cars drowned it out. "The bus," she screamed again, snapping Aaron to attention. She clambered around their vehicle. "We have to follow it, try to stop it."

Aaron was already running for the driver's seat of the rental. That's what she loved about him. When she needed him to move, there were no questions, no delays—he just moved.

The car raced toward a hundred kilometers per hour in seconds. Neither went for their seatbelts.

"Tell me about the prison bus," Aaron said. "Is it going to crash?" He glanced at her, then back at the road. "Is this a prison break thing?"

"Just get close," she said. "I'll ask Vivian."

She grabbed the car's owner's manual from the glove box and turned it over to a blank white page on the back. Pen in hand, she waited.

As if she was eighteen years old again, Sarah's eyes rolled back in her head, and she slumped in the car seat. A moment later, she blinked and sat up.

The blue bus was closer. Only three cars separated them from it, and the bridge parts trucks.

"What was that?" she asked Aaron, her heart racing. "What just happened to me?"

"It looked like you passed out. You haven't done that in ages."

When she passed out years ago, Vivian would use her hand to write prophecies and messages. Could she be doing that again? If so, why?

Sarah averted her gaze from the road. She had a pen in her hand but no paper. At her feet was the car's owner's manual, the glovebox gaping open.

Aaron changed lanes as she bent to retrieve the manual. The same manual she had in her lap moments before, poised to write on.

With a sideways glance to see if Aaron was watching her,

Sarah flipped the manual over. Her handwriting was clearly scrawled along the back of the small book.

Sarah gasped, dropping the manual back to the floor.

"What?" Aaron asked, his voice cracking.

The bus drew closer. One car separated them now. Aaron pulled out to pass the last car.

The bus swerved, then righted itself. It swerved again.

"There are thirteen men on that bus," Sarah said, her voice monotone. "Ten prisoners, two officers, and the driver."

"So, they're the thirteen we're supposed to save?"

"I'm not sure we can save them."

"What? Why?" Aaron revved the engine and came up alongside the bus, giving it a wide berth as it swerved again.

Sarah gripped the armrest and the console, her sister's words repeating in her head.

They'll blame you, Sarah. Let them die. It's the only way. They can't be saved. Sometimes fate wins ...

"Go," she said. "Get out of here." An exit came up on the right. "Take that exit. The Centre Street exit to Napanee. Get us as far from that bus as possible."

Aaron hugged the shoulder as the prison bus swerved into his lane. He was too close, though. Unable to avoid it, the bus clipped the side of their car. It wasn't enough to lose control, but enough to scrape some of the new car's paint job. Aaron stayed on the shoulder, then raced up the exit ramp, where he pulled over and stopped in a cloud of dust.

Sarah exited the car and watched as the bus was going too fast to manage another swerve across the lanes.

The bus had no brakes. Vivian knew everything, but her

messages came too late today.

The lines were cut at their last rest stop. Whoever cut the lines was gunning for Sarah. She was sure of it. But she had no idea how cutting brake lines on a prison bus would ever be connected to her.

Unable to slow down, the blue prison bus swerved one more time.

The driver lost control. The tires caught on the pavement. As if in slow motion, the bus swerved the opposite way, lifted sideways, and barrel-rolled several feet above the highway.

As Sarah watched with dread and fascination, the bus hit the ground and collapsed inward. Pieces of the vehicle sprayed like shrapnel, glass shattering along the body of the bus as it rolled again and again.

Brakes squealed from approaching vehicles as they attempted to stop in time.

A siren from behind the large bridge-part trucks wailed as a lone police cruiser approached on the shoulder at double the speed of traffic.

When the bus came to a complete stop on its side, crumpled and dented, Sarah leaned against the rental car, legs weakened by what she'd witnessed. So many dead. So much loss. Vivian warned her about the loss of life but then ordered her off.

Why Vivian? Why allow them to die?

All it did was firm up her decision to retire.

"Come on, Aaron," she said. "I've seen enough."

"Maybe we should go help them."

Sarah shook her head. "Vivian said they were headed to

Milhaven Maximum Security Prison. Let the authorities handle it. Look," she pointed, "they're already there."

Aaron glanced back at her. "They're people first, criminals second."

She stared at the police cruiser as it stopped by the bus. "I didn't mean it that way, and you know it."

A fire started near the front of the bus. Rescuers jumped back at a small explosion.

"People are going to burn to death," Aaron shouted.

"What do you want me to do about it?" Sarah screamed back at him.

"Obviously nothing," Aaron said, then ran toward the bus.

"Aaron!" she shouted after him. "Don't."

Then she, too, ran toward the burning bus.

Chapter 2

MARK RUSSELL STARED OUT the bus window, a cool sweat forming on his brow. His brother scared him. The look in his brother's eyes. The sorrow, the pain. A lot of what Rob had said didn't make much sense. At the rest stop, he was left to decipher his brother's words from moments ago.

"It's all her fault," Rob shouted through the bus's window. "I had no choice. Blame Sarah Roberts."

No choice? Blame Sarah Roberts?

What the hell did that mean? And why was his brother so stricken with fear?

Before all that, Mark had watched his brother pull into the rest stop behind the prison bus. Rob had gotten out of his police cruiser, leaned on the hood, and fiddled with a small device of some kind. From where Mark sat, he was sure it wasn't a cell phone, but he wasn't close enough to see exactly what his brother held with such rapt attention.

Rob pushed several buttons, looked up and down, and pushed more buttons. Mark was tempted to pound on the window and get his brother's attention, but whatever Rob was doing seemed important. Besides, he was following the bus to make sure Mark was processed with respect when he arrived at Milhaven. It had to be. What other reason would his brother have for driving so many hours out of Toronto?

Mark was drawn to the bus driver exiting the restaurant with a few coffees. When he glanced back at his brother by the police car, Rob held whatever it was in his hand slightly higher and pointed toward the bus. He pushed something on the unit with his free hand, then lowered his head.

A popping sound emitted from under the prison bus. No one else seemed to notice.

What had his brother done? Was he trying to break Mark free? Was the device connected to the bus in some way?

But then Rob glanced at the windows of the prison bus, starting at the front and working his way toward Mark. Their eyes met. And Rob dropped the device, his mouth gaping, forming the word, *No*.

Rob had braced himself against his cruiser, a hand back on the hood. Mouth agape, he blanched, his head moving back and forth in disbelief. It appeared to Mark that his brother was going through something akin to shock.

After a moment, Rob hustled over to the bus's window and shouted that it was all Sarah's fault. He had tears in his eyes.

What scared Mark was his brother's eyes. They seemed

filled with pain. Intense pain.

It wasn't Rob's fault Mark was sitting on a prison bus en route to Milhaven. It wasn't his fault Mark had done the things he'd done, lived the life he'd lived.

Years on the street did one of two things to a young man. It either beat him down until he succumbed and became a part of the streets. Drugs, violence, gangs, in and out of juvenile detention centers, and finally, incarceration in places like Milhaven Maximum Security Prison. Or it turned a man around. Made him yearn to be off the streets. Fixed him up just right.

Rob Russell, Mark's brother, had made it out. After their parents split up, the brothers hit the streets. Mark stayed there, but Rob didn't. And now Rob was a cop, and Mark was on a bus heading to the J Unit of the Milhaven prison, considered one of the most notorious units in the Canadian correctional system.

So how was that Sarah Roberts's fault? How could that possibly be?

Mark adjusted himself in the seat as he watched random houses flit by the window. It wasn't a girl who put him there. He knew the name Sarah Roberts. She was that woman in the news recently. The one being credited for the deaths of several important people in the organized crime world in Toronto.

He sat up straighter, the shackles on his wrists clinking. *Sarah Roberts.*

Why would his brother follow the prison bus in his cruiser, while on duty and in uniform, to say it wasn't his fault, and he had no choice? *Blame Sarah,* he'd said. It didn't make sense.

And what was in Rob's hand? What did he do to the bus?

Mark wiped his forehead and looked over his shoulder. His brother followed the bus about a dozen cars back. Mark straightened his legs as far as possible, the shackles on his ankles limiting movement. No one paid him any attention. The other prisoners languished in the heated bus, heads back, some sleeping, waiting for their trip to Hell.

Trepidation filled his stomach with acid. *Sarah Roberts*. She came after criminals. Mark Russell was a criminal—a *convicted* criminal—on a bus filled with other criminals. And his brother was unofficially escorting the prison bus. And his brother said it was Sarah's fault.

Why? Was Sarah Roberts after him?

Could that have anything to do with his brother's plea ten minutes earlier? Filled with a cryptic dread, Mark's knees bobbed up and down. What the hell was his brother talking about? Was Sarah after him? Was she trying to kill him? If so, why?

The bus picked up speed. Mark watched the road through the cage near the front. Up ahead, a rig with a pickup truck escort flashing yellow lights was carrying something large, like bridge spans. The bus driver changed lanes too quickly. He overcorrected, got the bus under control, then mumbled something to the armed guard beside him. The guard said something back to the driver, but Mark couldn't hear from his seat in the back. A general panic rippled through the men in front of him as some of them mumbled under their breath.

What the fuck's going on?

Mark turned back. His brother's cruiser was close,

watching.

Why the personal escort? Was Sarah Roberts going to try something on the way to Milhaven?

He pressed his cheek to the window glass. A car was parked on the shoulder up ahead. He focused on it as the bus driver jerked the wheel again. Sweat dripped into Mark's eyes. He blinked it away, watching the car as they were about to pass. A man and a woman talked outside the vehicle. Blonde hair. An image of Sarah Roberts came to him. If that woman standing by the car on the side of the road was Sarah … a sinking feeling consumed him.

It was Sarah. He was sure of it. And his brother had warned him.

The bus was passing the car now. The woman turned to him, her eyes locking with his.

Sarah Roberts, for sure.

He'd recognize her anywhere.

"It's her!" he shouted. "Sarah Roberts. She's going to kill us." Then he screamed, his face pressed into the glass as she was lost behind the bus.

A general uproar rose from his fellow prisoners. One of the guards shouted for calm.

Mark rose from his seat, his mouth dry, and pointed in Sarah's direction as the bus continued along the highway at an incredible speed. "It's Sarah's fault. It's all her fault."

"What the fuck you be talkin' 'bout?" a man two seats up asked.

The bus jerked to the left, then right again, knocking Mark back into his seat. The prison guard at the front of the bus yelled at the driver. Mark overheard the word *brakes* as he pressed his face against the glass again and watched Sarah fall farther behind them. He mumbled to himself, fear-driven gibberish.

It all came clear to him in moments. The bus didn't have brakes. Somehow, Sarah had disabled the brakes. And Rob, still trailing them, knew Sarah would do something to the bus, but he didn't know what. He followed, hoping to catch her in the act.

But Sarah was too good for all of them.

The bus swerved hard enough to knock Mark into the side wall. Despair filled him. They were going to die. Shackled, he couldn't do anything about it.

"We're all gonna die," he yelled. "It's Sarah's fault."

Someone shouted for him to shut the fuck up, but he kept his eyes on the bridge they were about to pass under.

His stomach clenched when the bus took a hard right, something most vehicles couldn't manage at that speed, and then lifted off the highway sideways. The sound of the tires ceased for a brief moment. A silence filled the interior of the bus. Seconds later, the bus smashed into the ground on its side, knocking its occupants downward in a bone-crushing thud. The prisoners' screams mixed with the hellish sound of protesting metal as the bus slid on the pavement.

Something clicked somewhere on the bus, and then there was a whoosh sound, like a lighter-fluid-soaked BBQ starting at the first touch of flame. Bright flames licked up from the engine and, like Lucifer's fingers, reached through the first half of the bus as it slid forward, directly into the fire from the engine.

Men screamed as they were burned alive. Mark screamed

at the back of the bus, the heat of the flames singeing his hair.

The horrific scraping of metal on concrete stopped suddenly. Mark clambered backward, fighting to get away from the flames that consumed the front half of the bus, men and all. The screams were of nightmare quality, something out of horror movies. At that moment, a random thought struck Mark: if he made it out of the bus alive, he would hear those screams in his head for the rest of his life.

The back window had busted outward in the crash. Mark scrambled toward it, then was held back a moment as one of the other prisoners crawled over him, his prison garb aflame at the lower legs.

"Get off me," Mark shouted, edging from under the large man. He coughed as acrid smoke filled his lungs. The flames drew closer, two seats away, edging toward him. Every prisoner and guard on the bus was either dead or on fire except for him.

At the back window, the other guy batted at his burning legs. "Help me, man," he shouted.

But Mark looked past the prisoner. The back window may have broken out, but they weren't going anywhere. All the windows were gated with a mesh to keep prisoners in. They were going to die in the bus, their fate sealed. There was no way out. The men with the keys at the front of the bus were dead.

The other prisoner turned away from Mark after dousing the flames on his legs, his hands raw and red from the effort, and shouted for help through the mesh of the back window.

Mark's heart raced in his throat, his stomach clenched again, and he vomited on the broken glass in front of his face.

He was going to die, and it was Sarah's fault. His brother wouldn't be able to get them out in time.

He curled his legs inward, away from the heat. A police car's siren wailed outside, and tires screeched to a halt near the bus.

He screamed. The only remaining prisoner screamed with him.

Someone started kicking at the mesh on the outside.

"I'll get you out, Mark," his brother shouted. "Hold on, buddy!"

The flames drew closer as Mark shouted, "Sarah Roberts is out there." His breath caught in his throat, and he coughed again. "She was watching from the side of"—he coughed—"the road. It's all Sarah's fault."

"What?" Rob shouted back. "Just hang on."

His brother continued to kick the mesh as the flames drew closer.

And Mark began to cry as he bargained with God under his breath, knowing it was too late for deals.

His fate was sealed.

As the flames caught his clothes, and he screamed until his last breath, all he heard was that incessant kicking.

His brother kicked the mesh and screamed alongside him.

But to no avail.

Chapter 3

SARAH CHASED AFTER AARON. When they were forty feet from the burning bus and the screams of the dying prisoners, she dove at Aaron's shoulders, wrapped her hands around him, and tackled him to the soft shoulder of the highway. He grunted under her hundred and forty pounds of tight and honed muscles as she landed on him.

She scrambled over him, positioning her body weight to keep Aaron from getting up.

"Listen," she shouted into his ear. He didn't resist her, his body going limp. He wouldn't dare use his martial arts skill to counter her moves. She faced him, an inch from his nose. "We need to get back in our car and leave."

"Sarah—"

"No," she stammered. "If we stay, I'm finished."

"Finished?"

She let him go and got to her feet, dusting her pants off. "Finished, as in, I'll be arrested for this." She pointed at the bus as others still ran toward it.

The cop car had stopped, and the officer kicked at the back door.

Someone screamed her name. From inside the bus. Something about her wanting to kill them all.

A quick glance at Aaron confirmed he heard it, too.

"We need to leave," she said, a steely resolve in her voice. "Now."

"Okay." Aaron nodded and got to his feet. He took her by the forearm. "No one noticed us. They're all focused on the accident."

They turned back toward their rental. The screams reached her, and her chest ached. She yearned to help, to do something, but Vivian grew more agitated.

People die every day. Sarah couldn't help everyone.

But this was something else. Someone on that bus had shouted her name. Was it the man who watched her as the bus passed them on the shoulder, his face pressed against the glass? What did he know about her? Why would he think she wanted to kill them?

Halfway to their rental car, she looked back at the bus as the screams died.

Flames licked out the back window now. The cop kicking at the bus had retreated, his hands in front of his face. The heat from the fire had to be intense that close up.

"C'mon, Sarah," Aaron said, tugging on her shirt. "If we're leaving, we need to do it now."

Before she turned back to Aaron, the cop looked at her. Their eyes locked. She knew him. She knew what he had done. The name *Rob Russell* whispered into her consciousness. *Murderer.* He'd cut the brake lines with some kind of remote device. His own brother was inside the bus. The emotion of losing a family member, the torment on Rob's face, was real.

He pointed at Sarah, his finger shaking. He raised his thumb in the universal shape of a gun, then lowered the thumb, sending Sarah a message.

Vivian told her how Rob would die. Sarah would have a chance to save him by warning Rob's sister. There was still time for everything to work out. Still time …

Sirens screamed in the distance. Aaron tugged at her again. She broke eye contact with Rob and turned back to their car. Everything in her soul yearned to stride up to Rob Russell, break one or two of his bones—an arm or maybe a leg—and then make a citizen's arrest for multiple counts of first-degree murder. But she couldn't arrest a cop at the scene of an accident that would be blamed on her. Explaining to other officers that her dead sister told her everything about Rob's involvement wouldn't work. In the end, she would be arrested. Rob, as well as anyone close enough to hear the screaming from inside the bus, would know it was *Sarah's fault*, as the dying man had said with his last breath.

Before getting in the car, she took one last look at the carnage on the highway. The flames were a dozen feet high above the bus's engine compartment.

No one inside the bus survived, Vivian said. *No one survived.*

Officer Rob Russell was nowhere to be found. His car was gone.

"Getting in?" Aaron asked from the driver's seat.

Sarah scanned the people crowded around the bus. The cop was gone. His cruiser moved behind a parked truck, catching her eye. Rob couldn't help the men on the bus, so he returned to his car.

To come after her.

He reversed away from the stopped traffic and drove onto the grassy median. The nose of the car angled toward Sarah and Aaron.

"Get in," Aaron shouted. "He's coming after us."

Sarah dropped in the passenger seat as Aaron hit the gas, the forward motion slamming her door shut beside her. The car jerked onto the exit ramp, their seats shuddering with the violence, and a moment later, they were headed south into the small city of Napanee.

Sarah looked out the back window. Rob's cruiser was a hundred yards behind them, lights flashing, siren wailing, gaining quickly.

"Lose him," Sarah yelled at Aaron. "At all costs."

Aaron pushed the car hard as Sarah turned back in her seat and yanked the gas receipt from her pocket.

It's fate. All thirteen are supposed to die.

"Fuck," Sarah shouted, then crumpled up the receipt and tossed it over her shoulder.

Aaron took a hard right onto a road leading into a copse of trees. He took the first left.

Sarah checked the back window again. "We lose him in the next few minutes, and we're good. There hasn't been enough time for backup to get into position. Everyone's heading to the accident on the highway."

Aaron turned another corner. The pursuing cruiser lost sight.

Sarah righted herself in her seat, Vivian's presence close, then lost consciousness.

When she woke, the car was cruising at the posted speed limit. She had a pen and the car's owner's manual in her hand.

"What the hell?" she whispered.

Aaron glanced over at her. "You're back."

She dropped the pen and peeked at the message from Vivian.

"We lost him a couple of minutes ago," Aaron said. "Now I'm heading into Kingston on this side road. Once there, we'll dump this car and call Parkman. He can rent us a car in his name so we can continue wherever we're going."

"Yes," Sarah said in a daze, still feeling like Vivian had control of her. "Call Parkman."

"You okay?"

She looked at him, wishing it was all over and they were still headed to their vacation. She missed Drake. She missed Spencer. There would be no help from Darwin this time. It was her, Aaron, and Parkman. Vivian, too.

Someone had betrayed Sarah, and now they would blame the prison bus accident on her. All this, according to Vivian.

Aaron snuck glances at her. "Sarah? You're scaring me. Say something."

"Call Parkman."

"I heard that part. Say something else."

She held up the owner's manual. "Vivian said a lot here."

"Like what? Read it to me."

"She said we have to call Parkman. To warn him."

"Warn him? About what?"

"I'm not sure. She said I've been betrayed."

Aaron frowned. "How so?" He checked the mirrors, put on the blinker, and turned at a set of lights. "No one we know would betray you."

"Those prisoners in that bus …"

"What about them?" Aaron asked, looking at her, back at the road, then back to her again. "Tell me."

"They died because of me."

"That doesn't make sense."

"Vivian said it'll be blamed on me. I'm a vigilante known to the media. Instead of stopping the bad guys in the act, I've escalated to killing convicted criminals. That bus was headed to a maximum-security prison here in the Kingston area. Vivian showed me a mental picture of tomorrow's newspapers. The accident will be blamed on me. Beside my picture, it will say the authorities are looking to question me as a person of interest. They'll add the bit about me being seen at the accident and how I fled the area."

"You've killed people in the past, but you're no murderer. Anyone who knows you knows that's not possible. I mean, I know how that sounds, but you don't kill in cold blood. You just don't. And you had nothing to do with that accident other than the foreknowledge that it would happen."

Even with the air conditioning on full, Sarah felt overheated. She pulled her shirt away from her skin and shook it back and forth, fanning air under it.

"Okay, what do we do?" Aaron asked. "Has Vivian told you how to turn this around?"

Sarah nodded. "She has. But it doesn't make much sense right now."

"What's she saying?"

"Get back to Toronto."

"And do what?"

"Lie low. Help people with small issues. Like in the beginning, when I was eighteen. She'll tell me where to be and when. Give it time. This'll all work out, she says." Sarah paused. "But there's one more thing."

"I don't like the sound of that. What one more thing?"

Sarah held up the owner's manual and read the words Vivian wrote with Sarah's fingers.

"Vivian said I have to die for this to all go away."

"How many times have I heard that? No big issue. You've died before. Like in Denmark." Aaron looked at her, then back at the road. "You don't mean *die* for real, do you?"

"I'm not sure. I can tell you I won't live life on the run, off the grid. In this day and age, that's almost impossible."

"Look, whatever's going on, we can fix it. You have friends in high places." He tapped her leg. "Everything'll work out. I'm sure of it."

"Aaron, something else is bothering me."

"What is it?"

"Why's Vivian making me black out again? She's in my head. She can talk to me at any time, yet she's made me black out twice now. Why?"

Aaron shrugged, but she could tell it bothered him, too.

How would she tell him the rest of the message Vivian

had whispered to her? How would he take it?

Scuba diving lessons? Rent a boat? Make sure the world knows when Sarah is dead?

It's the only way, Sarah. You're in too deep this time.

When they got back to Toronto, she would tell him the rest. She would tell Parkman, too. They were out of options. Both men had to know everything Vivian had told her.

She didn't need Vivian to tell her that both men were going to hate the message.

Sarah hated it.

Chapter 4

Detective Joel Blacken stared out his office window at the restaurant on the other side of the alley, his mind racing with possibilities. Could he pull it off? Was the plan sound? Could he rely on Russell to do as he was told?

The private investigator he'd hired was worth every penny. The information he had would ruin careers and destroy marriages. The evidence in his desk drawer was enough to kill for, and kill was what he would have to do to protect himself.

There was no other way out.

He opened the desk drawer and stared at the picture, rancor rising in his throat. They would pay for what they did to him. They would all pay, and Sarah Roberts would help him deal with it. She would have no choice. He'd learned all he needed to know about Sarah while she was in Toronto recently. All the cops and detectives talked. He had everything, even Sarah's cell phone number. His friend had escorted Sarah and Aaron from the hospital to their home to pack their bags. Blacken even knew the route Sarah took to leave the city.

He knew everything.

"In time," he whispered in the empty office. "In time."

Gently, he set the photo back in his desk drawer, arranged the file he was working on—due that afternoon—under the picture, then closed the drawer, locked it, and pocketed the key.

The cell phone in his other pocket vibrated. The burner phone on his desk remained silent. He stared at the burner phone, willing it to ring as his personal cell vibrated again.

"Fuck."

He answered the vibrating phone with a grunt without bothering to look at the caller display.

"It's over." His wife.

"What on earth are you on about now, Kymberly? What's over?"

"Us. Everything. All over, Joel. I'm leaving you."

Joel shot up from his chair, gripping the phone tighter. "You're what?" He clenched his teeth so hard his jaw ached. Those few words sent his plan spiraling out of control.

"It's been over for years now, Joel. Don't give me your usual bullshit. You know it. I know it."

"You can't walk out now." He panted, gasping air in gulps. He was so close to finishing. One week. Maybe two. Then she could leave. *Permanently.*

"What?" she asked. "What's that supposed to mean?"

He fought to keep his voice under control as his rage seethed. "I … I mean, why now? Let's talk it over, figure things out."

"We've tried talking, Joel. You talk, but you don't listen. We've been at this for a decade and are both unhappy. Goodbye. I'll be at my sister's place—"

"Wait! Not today. You can't do this today." He hated the pleading tone in his voice. "Wait until next week. Don't move out. We'll deal with whatever's bothering you—"

"I'm packed and leaving in thirty minutes. And Joel?"

He would kill her with his bare hands. He would do it himself instead of getting Sarah to do it. Kym had changed the timetable and disrupted the plan. It had to be now. There was no other way.

"What?" he asked, surprised by how calm his voice sounded.

"Don't follow me. Don't come to my sister's place. You will hear from my lawyer. I want half of everything, or more, if my lawyer can work it out. Goodbye, Joel."

The line cut off before he could reply.

His hand snapped into a fist. He smashed the top of his desk.

"You fucking bitch," he spat out. "Fuck you. Whore!"

He dropped the cell in his pocket, snatched the burner phone off the desk, and bolted out of his office. He'd find her. He'd detain her. Tie her up for a week if he has to because she can't leave him yet. It had to be on his terms, his way. Then she could leave him. She could leave this world, too, for all he cared.

The office bustled around him as he passed colleagues and friends. He heard nothing and responded to no one as he jogged toward the elevators. He would drive home and catch Kym before she left. He would convince her to stay, or he would make her stay.

Either way, Kymberly wasn't leaving him.

No fucking way in hell.

Chapter 5

Sarah and Aaron returned the car to a rental agency, took a Kingston bus across town, and rented a different car using Benjamin's credit card. Aaron neglected to tell Benjamin they'd be upgrading to an SUV. Benjamin wouldn't mind because they would pay him back—eventually. To be safe, Aaron had gone in to rent the car alone while Sarah waited in a small café a block away. If the authorities were looking for them, they'd have Sarah's description, name, and the fact that she's with her boyfriend. Benjamin renting a car online for his friend wouldn't raise red flags. Aaron was just picking up the car, so the attendant photocopied his license without a glance and handed over the keys.

They had tried Parkman's cell number but couldn't reach him.

Now, as the air conditioning cooled the large interior of the Escalade, they passed the small city of Oshawa. After Whitby, Ajax, and Pickering, they'd head south on the Don Valley Parkway through Scarborough and into Toronto, hoping to rendezvous with Parkman.

"Try him again," Aaron said. "I hope he hasn't left yet."

Sarah sat up straighter. "He said something about heading back to Santa Rosa." She dialed his number for the third time. "You think he booked a ticket and has already left the country?" She put the phone to her ear. Before Aaron could answer, she said, "Too soon. He would've taken a room for the night. He's probably sleeping after everything that happened over the past week." The phone rang, unanswered at Parkman's end.

"Does Vivian know anything?" Aaron asked.

Sarah pursed her lips and blew out a small puff of air. "Pfft, she's all quiet now." She set the phone in her lap, staring out the windshield at nothing. "You don't think something happened to him, do you?"

"Parkman?" Aaron glanced at her, then back at the road. "No way. Not Parkman."

"True."

As buildings passed her window, she thought about what Vivian had said about a betrayal. *A vile betrayal.* Who would do that to her? Who *could*? And why would that someone feel the need to betray her? Had she wronged them in some way?

It couldn't be anyone close to her. Parkman, Darwin, Aaron's teachers, Daniel, Alex, or Benjamin. None of them would go against her for any personal gain. Then who? And if it wasn't someone close, could it be called a betrayal? Wasn't that just someone angry with her, out to get her?

"What're you thinking about?" Aaron asked.

"Something Vivian said."

"Like what?"

She turned to face him. "The betrayal thing."

"Wait for it. Deal with it, then. Wracking your brain to *think* about who it might be and what they might have done is a waste of time. Anyway, no one close to you would ever dream of betraying you."

"I thought of that." She grabbed the cell phone and dialed Parkman again. No answer. "I'm worried about him."

"Don't be." Aaron changed lanes to pass a slow-moving truck. "Parkman can handle himself." Aaron glanced in the rearview mirror, back at the road, then in the mirror again.

"What?" Sarah asked. "What is it?"

"I think we're being followed."

Sarah tried to use the side mirror outside her door but couldn't get a good look behind them. She spun in her seat. Two cars back, the red and blue light casing on the roof of a police cruiser was almost completely hidden behind a pickup truck.

"Can you lose them?"

"I'm going to try."

Aaron signaled and changed lanes to the right, then exited off the express lanes and onto the collector lanes.

"Did he follow?" she asked, gripping her cell phone tightly.

"Yes, he did."

"Shit."

She raised the phone and dialed.

"Who're you calling?"

"Casper. We had nothing to do with that bus accident, and he's got the power to get the assholes behind us off our tail."

"Smart thinking."

Casper answered on the second ring.

"It's Sarah. We may have a problem."

"Talk to me."

"We're being followed by a cruiser on the 401, and we don't know why. Is it one of your people?"

"No."

"We think it's tied to that prison bus accident near Napanee today."

"Why? Did you cause it? Were you there?"

"We had nothing to do with it. But Vivian told me about it, and Aaron and I stopped to see what we could do. One of the dying prisoners yelled my name."

"Odd. Anything else?"

"Yeah, get these guys off our ass."

"Get me a plate number."

Sarah turned to Aaron. "Slow down. Get closer to the cruiser. I need a plate number." Then she spoke into the phone. "You need anything else? Like a number on the side of the vehicle?"

"No. The plate will tell me who it's assigned to."

When they were close enough, Sarah read the plate number to him.

"Got it. I'll call you back."

Aaron resumed speed while Sarah adjusted the side

mirror to watch the cruiser.

"We'll just sit tight until Vivian tells me what the hell's going on."

"I'm not leading this guy to my place or the new dojo."

"If he's still on our ass when we get downtown, just keep driving. Don't exit the highway. Casper will handle it."

"How?"

"I have no idea."

She dialed Parkman again. Still no answer.

Chapter 6

JOEL'S PALM WAS NUMB from slamming it into the steering wheel on the drive to his house. He worked downtown and had to drop onto the Gardiner Expressway to leave the base of Toronto, heading west through Etobicoke, which took him through the lower part of Mississauga and into the small but pretty area of Port Credit. In the middle of the afternoon, he could do it in thirty minutes, but today, he'd gotten to his house in less than twenty-four minutes.

His wife's car wasn't in the driveway.

She'd already left.

His cell phone rang. He snatched it out of his pocket and checked call display.

His boss, Sergeant Travis Jensen. "Fuck! Not now." He slammed the phone on the passenger seat. "Fitting that you should call right now, asshole."

He continued up the drive and parked at the front door. Leaving the car running, he got out and checked the door. Locked. He peeked through the window. Kym was gone.

He jumped back in the car and hit the gas. Kym's sister lived in Oakville. Maybe if he gunned it along Lakeshore Road, he could beat her there.

Determined to reach Kym before she got to her sister's place, he pushed his car to its limits, passing other vehicles recklessly. It was dangerous and stupid, but if Kym got away from him, he couldn't follow through with his plans. Everything would fall apart, and he would lose more money than Kym ever dreamed about. In fact, it was so much money it was worth more to him than she was.

"Why this week, Kym?" Joel said out loud, the strain in his voice surprising him. "Why did you go and do it this week? You could've waited just seven more days. Just one more ..."

He ran a yellow light that turned red before he got through the intersection and kept going. He dared a cop to try and pull him over. He would produce his own detective ID and get the officer's badge number. There were things he could do to a traffic cop that would make that cop want to choose another career.

His cell rang again. He checked the clock on the dash. It's at least ten more minutes to Kym's sister's place.

With a single button push, his phone connected to the car stereo via Bluetooth, and his boss coughed.

"Jensen," he said, his tone curt, all business. "It's Blacken. What's up?"

"That report is due today. The gang unit needs your criminal informant's intel before they do their thing."

Joel frowned. "Their thing? Aren't they doing that on the weekend?"

"Nope. Been moved up. Doing it tomorrow. I need that file now."

"When I get back to the office, I'll bring it up."

The incriminating picture was on top of the file in his desk. If Sergeant Jensen had seen the picture, all would have been lost. If his wife left him today, all would be lost. And if Rob Russell didn't call him soon with the results on the prison bus, all would be lost.

He smashed the steering wheel twice.

"Blacken, I need it now. Just tell me where it is, and you can add whatever you need to it when you return. The men are in the conference room. They're waiting. This is a go. Now."

"It's locked in my desk. I've got the key."

"How long before you're back?"

"Not sure. A couple of hours."

"Not good enough, Blacken. You told me you were office-bound today. I told them the same. The gang unit needs that file. It can't wait. I'll have maintenance open the lock. No need to worry—"

"No!" Joel shouted. *The picture.* "Do not go into my desk."

There was a moment's pause, then his sergeant said, "I caution you, Blacken. Your tone, your aggression must be reined in." He cleared his throat. "This is police property. Police business. I have men's lives at stake here, and you're sitting on a report that could save lives. Either you're opening this desk for me within five minutes, or I'm having maintenance do it. Is that understood?"

This desk. Like his boss was standing in his office. Was Jensen in his space?

"Are you in my office?" Blacked asked.

"Yes. I came looking for you and the file."

Blacken swallowed, then licked his lips. Why was everything falling apart when he was so close?

"Get out of my office, Jensen. I will only warn you once."

"Detective Blacken. I will remind you to curtail your insubordinate tone, or there *will* be consequences. If you want me out of your office, open this desk, give me the file, and I will leave your office."

"Jensen, I will—"

"You will do no such thing because you can't get back in time. I'm hanging up now to call maintenance. If I don't find the file, there will be disciplinary actions. You have a job to do, Blacken, and I expect you to do it."

The line went dead.

"Fuck," Blacken shouted. He punched the dash twice, the car swerving into the oncoming lane and then back into his. "Fuck you, Jensen."

It was all unraveling. Too quick. He knew exactly why Jensen was being a hard ass. Because he'd been fucking Kymberly for months. The same reason Kym was leaving him.

Maybe he'd waited too long to get things rolling. He had needed time to think and figure out how to make things right.

With the proof of infidelity weighing him down and the excitement of newfound money through his gang activity payoffs, his head was all over the place. His plan had holes in it. But he could work with it, change as things happened, roll with the punches. He really needed Russell to get back to him about the prison bus and not do anything stupid.

It was too late to stop Jensen. He would open the desk, see the picture, and know what Blacken knew.

They had hit the point of no return.

For the next week, Blacken would appear to be doing his job. He would avoid Jensen at all costs. He would write a complaint about Jensen for his behavior regarding Mrs. Kymberly Blacken, a fellow detective's wife, and he would wait. At the end of the week, when every cop in North America was hunting Sarah Roberts, he would call her to offer a way out. An honorable way out.

The burner phone rang.

He snatched it up. "Talk to me."

Russell was crying on the other end of the line. "It's done."

"Then why are you crying?"

"My brother's dead."

"Your brother? How's that possible?" Blacken's mind raced. How did Rob get that close to the bus? He wasn't supposed to see his brother.

"He was on the bus."

"What? Really?"

"Sentenced to Milhaven," Russell wailed, his voice rising. "I saw him at the gas station. It was too late." He sobbed. "You knew."

Lie to him? Or tell him the truth? Which way kept Russell under better control?

He decided on the brutal truth.

"Price of admission." Russell knew too much. He had a debt. Sabotaging the bus's brakes was his debt fulfilled. Killing his own brother was his silence ensured. "Where are you?" Blacken negotiated a turn, slowed for a yield sign, and squawked his tires as he raced along Speers Road. Less than two minutes from Apryl's house. Kym's sister lived alone. As an exec at an investment firm in Toronto, Apryl worked from her two-story Victorian home in Oakville. There was plenty of room for Kym, but she wouldn't be staying. Not if Joel had anything to say about it.

"I'm done," Russell said. "I'm out."

"Out? What do you mean, out? You can't leave now. In fact, you don't get to leave. That's not how this shit works."

"I already left. Dropped off my cruiser, handed in my duty belt, left my letter of resignation, and drove away in my civilian vehicle."

"All because your brother died? Wow, I mean, I've heard grief affects us all in different ways, but that takes the cake."

Russell's voice was still shaky when he said, "This isn't just grief. This is guilt, too. My brother didn't just die. I *killed* him."

"Accidentally."

"Spin it any way you want. It all comes out the same. I killed my brother, and now I have to pay for that."

Blacken slowed the car and edged to the curb three houses from Apryl's. "What do you mean you have to pay for it?"

The pause was so long that Blacken thought Russell had set down the phone.

"I won't tell anyone about you, Blacken. I won't talk. But you won't ever see me again. You're a disease, and you're contagious."

"Lie to me, lie to yourself. But remember, every day while you're on the run, it's all just lies you're telling yourself. This has nothing to do with me or your brother and everything to do with your gambling debts. You owe powerful people a lot of money, and now you're running. That's what this is. Tell me I'm wrong."

"Goodbye, Blacken."

"If you run, you're as good as dead, Russell—"

The line died.

Would anything go his way? At that moment, Jensen was probably staring at the picture of himself wearing a dog collar while Blacken's wife, Kymberly, bounced on him.

There was one thing for sure. He was in too deep to too many people to pull back now. Grab his wife, keep her to himself for at least a week, and everything would work out.

He watched Apryl's house. No movement anywhere. No vehicles. He drove up the half-moon driveway and parked. Unless they'd hidden Kym's Jeep, she wasn't here.

He dialed Apryl's home number and got voicemail. No one was home.

Where could Kym be?

His phone rang: Jensen.

"Fuck you," he said to the phone without answering it. "Enjoy the photo, asshole."

Then it came to him: Kymberly lied. She wasn't going to

stay with her sister. She was going to stay at Jensen's place. She was moving in with her boyfriend.

Blacken performed a U-turn and headed back to Toronto, to Jensen's place. Jensen wouldn't be there. He was breaking into Blacken's desk.

Kymberly wouldn't see him coming.

He gripped the steering wheel tighter and shoved the accelerator to the floor, blocking all thoughts of Rob Russell from his mind.

Chapter 7

PARKMAN STEPPED OUT OF the yoga studio and turned on his cell phone. He'd wanted to start yoga for some time but had never gotten around to it. He'd been busy with Sarah, and now that it was *me* time, he wanted to exercise routinely. Since there was some time before he had to be at the airport, the ninety-minute workout and cleansing swim had done wonders for him. Refreshed and ready for his flight to Los Angeles, he stowed his bag in the back of the rental and got in, tossing his phone in the seat beside him.

After several years of traversing the world, he felt restless. Would private security work satisfy him? He'd been doing it off and on for quite some time, but if that was all he had to do, would he feel sated?

He pulled into traffic on Airport Road, mentally noted his

terminal number, and wondered if Sarah was truly finished with Vivian. Could she just vacation? Or was Sarah ready to retire?

How would she find satisfaction, get to a place of being sated herself? Family life could possibly do it. A child, a house, a mortgage. Perhaps.

Somehow, he didn't see Sarah Roberts settled down. Aaron, yes, but not Sarah.

Unless Vivian went quiet. Then maybe.

Parkman signaled to turn left but was cut off by a dark pickup. He jerked back into his lane, waited for the pickup to pass—a curse word on his lips—then eased into the turn lane.

The pickup driver stopped at the red light, then spun in his seat to look back at Parkman.

Parkman raised his hands and mouthed the word, *What?*

The driver faced forward.

"What the hell, man," Parkman said to the empty car. "You cut me off."

The light changed. The pickup pulled forward and entered the airport parking for Terminal Three. Parkman followed as the rental car agency parking area was straight ahead.

After several openings to the lot, the pickup truck veered to the left and disappeared along an aisle.

Parkman continued forward and parked in a marked car-rental spot. He gathered his phone, slipped it into his back pocket, grabbed his stuff from the back seat, quickly scanned the vehicle, and locked it.

He returned the key and signed their documents inside the car rental office.

The young clerk—had to be no older than twenty-two—smiled at Parkman. "Thank you, sir, for renting with us. We hope to see you again soon."

Parkman returned the smile. "I don't think so. Not this time." He moved toward the door. "I'm going to miss Toronto, but I don't see myself back here for quite some time."

"Well," the clerk collected the paperwork and the pen from the top of the desk, "we'd be happy to see you when you do return, sir. Have a safe flight."

Parkman offered the young man a smile and nodded, then stepped from the tiny office. He shouldered his bag and started toward the terminal.

"Parkman," a man said. "Over here."

He swung to the left, then the right.

"This way," the man said.

Parkman went left again. The pickup truck. The one who cut him off. The driver's side window was open, the man's arm hanging out.

Parkman stepped forward. "How do you know my name?"

The driver waved for him to come closer. Something in his gut cautioned him, but he continued forward anyway.

"What's going on?" It was all he could think to ask.

"I've done something," the man said. "Something evil."

Parkman drew closer still. The look in the man's eyes was fear. There was pain written all over his face.

"Call a priest," Parkman said.

"I can't call anyone."

Parkman stopped a couple of feet from the open window.

"Why's that?"

Distraught, the man looked down at his lap. "I did things. Terrible things." He glanced up through his windshield, his eyes glazed over. "Things I can't come back from. I was warned, but I did it anyway."

"Why tell me?"

"Because I'm supposed to arrest you on some trumped-up charge to get you off the street. I won't do it, though. You're the only one who can help her."

"Arrest me? Help her?" His mind raced to Sarah. "Do you mean Sarah?"

The man spoke before Parkman could ask him more.

"I've seen things."

He had Parkman's attention now. "What kind of things?"

A car approached. The man watched a Ford Taurus ease closer.

"Unspeakable things."

The man was talking in circles. They weren't getting anywhere.

"How do you know my name?" Parkman asked. "Tell me more about the trumped-up charge shit."

The Ford passed them, not losing any speed. The man's gaze followed the car, then stopped on Parkman's face.

"I know the hotel you were in. I watched you enter the yoga studio. I know your flight, even the flight number."

Parkman's gut cautioned him further. He eased the bag off his shoulder. "And how would you know all of that?"

"We *all* know it. We know where Sarah is, too. And Aaron."

"You might want to start by telling me who the fuck you

are?" Parkman was losing his patience with the man's game. He edged closer to get a look inside the pickup. The man's right hand hadn't been visible since they began talking. That didn't bode well. In fact, no part of the situation boded well for any of them. "Are you with any of the seven families in Toronto?" Parkman asked, thinking this might be connected to what Sarah had just dealt with in Toronto.

The man shook his head. "No, nothing like that. But it might as well be."

"Then what's this all about? Why would anyone track us so closely?" He checked his watch. "I have a plane to catch," he added, wondering if he would be leaving after all.

The driver of the pickup checked his mirrors. He glanced over Parkman's shoulder, then back at Parkman.

"I've done things—"

"We've covered that," Parkman interrupted.

"—and to fix those things, I had to do one more thing."

"You're not making any sense."

"There's no escape for me." The man's eyes turned from fear to despair to desperation. He came across as genuinely scared. "I'm in too deep. I've crossed the line. There's no way out." He sat up in his seat and wiped his nose with his right hand. Parkman was relieved to see it was weaponless.

He also saw what the man was wearing. "Kevlar?"

The driver looked down, then back at Parkman. "I'm a dead man. They're looking for me." His voice broke and trembled.

"You're here for help?"

He shook his head slowly. "You have to warn Sarah."

Parkman stepped closer. Those words pissed him off.

"Warn Sarah about what?"

"Just warn her. The Blacken has plans, and people get hurt when the Blacken has plans."

"What's *the Blacken*?"

"You'll know soon enough." The driver turned on the truck.

"Wait." Parkman put a hand on the door. "Don't leave. You can't leave. Explain this to me. Nothing makes sense. You're on the run, presumably for your life, and I'm to warn Sarah because the Blacken has plans. Great. And what do I tell Sarah? Watch out for the Blacken? That'll go over well."

The man leaned closer to Parkman, the intensity in his face going up a notch. "Blacken is a man's name. I've said enough already." He glanced around again as if someone watched them. "I've seen things cops have done. I've been involved. I owe money. To pay my debt, I took out that prison bus so it would look like Sarah did it. To silence me, they made sure my brother was on that bus. They made me murder my own brother."

"What are you saying? What bus?"

"You'll hear about it soon. But listen, Sarah was there. She saw it. After giving a half-assed chase, I booted back to my department, dropped off my cruiser, and drove to the yoga studio where my colleagues told me you were. So here I am, warning you to warn Sarah." He smacked Parkman's hand off the door. "Get the fuck out of Toronto. Leave the country. All of you. Take Aaron. Blacken's plans only work if you stay or if Sarah stays."

"Okay, I'm willing to tell Sarah that, but if you know anything about Sarah, she'll leave or stay because she wants to, not because someone warned her. Not even me."

"Then it'll be her death."

"And what're you going to do? You think this Blacken is after you?"

The man nodded. "Oh, he's after me. No question. But I'll find him first. I know where he stays. I know his places."

The truck edged forward a foot.

"Wait. Can I get a name?"

The man looked back. "Death," he said, then wiped his watery eyes and drove away, his tires protesting at the first corner.

"What the fuck?" Parkman whispered.

He retrieved his cell phone. Twelve missed calls and seven messages.

"What the fuck?" he said again.

On the side, the button to mute the phone had been pressed. He hated the vibrate option, so his phone had been muted all morning. He had muted it before bed and left it muted while in the yoga studio.

All twelve calls from Sarah.

He dialed her back and checked his watch again. If he was flying out, he had to enter the terminal, but something told him he would stay in Toronto longer.

"Parkman," Sarah's voice. "Finally."

"What's up?"

"Listened to any of my messages?" she asked, her tone anxious, clipped.

"Not yet. The phone was on mute. I'm at the airport and just met with a strange, paranoid man who spoke about a prison bus—"

"Parkman?"

"Yeah."

"Meet us at the hotel."

"Which hotel?"

"Not sure. Pick one. Book a room. Then text me, and we'll meet you there."

He turned back and looked at the car rental office. "Why is everything so strange today?"

"You'll get a room? Then text it?"

"Location preference?"

"Near the airport."

"You're close to the airport?"

"Minutes away."

"I'll text you back in a sec."

He shut down his phone, walked over, and entered the car rental office.

The clerk's face lit up. "Back so soon?"

Chapter 8

Blacken approached Jensen's house from the rear. He'd parked a block away, ensuring Kymberly wouldn't see his car or see him coming. The more he thought about it, the more he knew Kymberly had to be at Jensen's.

Jensen lived just north of Toronto in Barrie. The house was on the south edge of town, the property backing onto environmentally protected land. That allowed Blacken to use trails to get behind Jensen's house. Once he was in the trees, he could watch the rear of the house for movement. It wouldn't do well to storm a house filled with Jensen's relatives from out of town or something of that nature. Not only would his career be over, but his wife would still be gone.

On the forty-minute drive north from the top of Toronto,

Blacken called his media contact, Blair Mackey. He explained they had enough evidence to prove Sarah Roberts was responsible for the prison bus accident, but it wasn't *officially* announced yet. Also, his wife was missing. An official missing person's report would be filed later that day, but he also thought Sarah had something to do with that as well.

Blair said he'd go with the story.

"And share it with whomever you want," Blacken said. "Tell everyone we must apprehend Sarah Roberts as soon as possible."

He'd also called in a BOLO—Be On The Lookout—for Sarah Roberts. It would give him great pleasure to apprehend her himself, but he knew that was unlikely. As long as the authorities held her, he could get to her and realize his plan.

But first, he had to get his wife back. For everything to work, he couldn't let Kymberly slip away.

The late afternoon sun had a ways to go before it set, but it was already behind the stand of tall trees surrounding Jensen's house, casting the back windows in shadow. This made seeing inside much easier.

After checking his phone several times, Blacken waited. He watched and waited.

After a fifteen-minute wait, he was rewarded.

Kymberly, his beloved wife, strode into Jensen's kitchen, wine glass in one hand, her cell phone in the other. After filling her glass, she left the kitchen and disappeared deeper inside the house.

"Bitch," he whispered as he edged out from behind the tree and made his way to the eight-foot fence.

If a neighbor saw him and came out to confront him, he'd simply show his detective ID and tell them to remain inside their home as he was about to arrest a suspect.

He'd seen no movement in the neighbors' homes on either side, though. Curtains were drawn, and lights were off in both cases. He and his wife were alone as Jensen was still in Toronto.

His gun holstered—he wouldn't need it for his wife—he climbed over the back fence, ran to the house, and placed his back to the brick wall. A moment later, after catching his breath, he tried the sliding door into the basement.

Unlocked.

What an idiot.

He slid it open slowly until there was enough room to squeeze inside, then soundlessly eased it back in place. He'd done this sort of thing for years as a detective. Raided homes with addicts and bank robbers. And even though there was no real danger here, his heart still raced with the stealth, beating its rhythm in his ears.

He took a calming breath and started for the stairs. At the base of the stairs, his wife's voice was barely audible. She had to be on the third floor. The circular stairwell spiraled up the center of the house. From the basement, he could see the banisters all the way to the top.

He tested each step for creaks before committing his weight. On the next floor, the kitchen sat to his right, living room to his left. Kymberly's voice echoed throughout the house from one floor above.

He shuffled quietly along the tile floor to where the stairs started upward again, then began to climb with less worry. If she heard him now, the only person who would hear her shout would be whomever she was talking to on the phone.

Halfway up, he tuned into her side of the conversation. She was talking about *their* house. Something about market value. How much she would get, and why she had to settle for only half.

It had to be her lawyer. The marriage wasn't even over. It had only been a few hours since she'd called to tell him she was done, and she was already trying to fuck him over.

His anger stirred to rage and justified his plans for her. If only she'd waited a week longer.

No matter. He'd make it work regardless. Maybe he'd even be able to figure out something for Jensen. An accident, perhaps.

At the top of the stairs, he stopped.

Something moved in the room to his right. Kymberly was in the room on his left as her whiny voice reached a new pitch. She rambled on about their assets and how she wanted the investment portfolio to be divided with the least amount of tax responsibility.

Blacken waited, his back to the wall. He gripped the butt of the weapon in its holster, not sure if he should have it out or not. What if Jensen had a brother? Someone to look after Kym?

He had known Jensen for several years, and he'd never mentioned a brother.

After several seconds, his wife's voice droning on in the other room, his hand lowered from the holster. He pushed away from the wall and peeked inside the room behind him. The master bedroom was empty, just a large bed with end tables and a dresser.

He exhaled and turned around.

Kymberly stood at the door to the room, her mouth open.

"I'll have to call you back. Something's come up." She ended the call and lowered the phone.

This was his moment. The jockey crossing the finish line, the beaten fighter coming back to win with a knockout. He wanted to take a few seconds to revel in it. She had cheated. He'd hired an investigator, and now he had pictures. She had fucked him over. Just when his time was coming, his big break was something she could have enjoyed as well. If only she'd been a proper wife to him.

Kym should have known him by that point. After all their years together, she should've known.

Nobody fucks with Blacken.

Nobody.

Or they got hurt.

She took a step closer and coughed into her hand. "What the fuck is this? You're trespassing." She raised a finger. "No, wait, this is a break and enter." She wagged that finger back and forth, a demon smile crossing her lips, eyes narrowed. "You're finished, Joey. When Jensen hears about this, you're through, you *bastard*."

Blacken stared at her a moment longer, allowing the edge of a smile to curl his lips.

"You're the worst kind of human, you know that." He took a step toward her. She coughed again. "I heard you on the phone, trying to fuck me over. You can't just leave and make it fair. You have to try to ruin me in the process."

"How did you know to come here?" she shouted, spittle

shooting from her mouth. The color came to her face whenever she was enraged. "How'd you figure it out?"

"Private investigator. I've got pics." Five feet from her, he stopped and crossed his arms, nodding. "And the judge will see all of the evidence of your infidelity with my boss. There goes Jensen's credibility."

"You bastard," she shrieked. "I'll kill you."

"Not if I kill you first, cheating whore."

He lunged at her.

Chapter 9

AT A TIM HORTON'S coffee shop near the airport, Sarah kept herself hidden in a corner booth, and Aaron placed himself in a way that prevented people from seeing Sarah's face. They nursed two large coffees and waited for Parkman to text them with the hotel information.

"Is there anything else Vivian told you?" Aaron asked.

Sarah nodded. "Plenty, but I'd rather only have to say it once. As soon as we're with Parkman, I'll explain everything."

"How bad?"

"Aaron … please."

"That bad, eh?"

She met his gaze. "It'll be okay. We've been through worse."

Her phone dinged. Parkman. Holiday Inn by Highway 427. Room 216.

"Got it. Let's go."

"How far?" Aaron asked.

"Two minutes."

They drove over without incident, parked, and entered the hotel lobby. Once on the elevator, Aaron placed his hands in his pocket. A gesture that meant, she had learned, he was nervous.

"It'll be okay, Aaron. Really." She held out a hand. He pulled out his left hand and held hers as the elevator door opened on the second floor. "As long as you two trust me." They stepped off the elevator. "And Vivian."

"You know we do. It's fate I don't trust."

They started along the corridor to room 216.

"What do you mean by fate?"

"You can't keep doing what you do without something going horribly wrong at some point. We're good now. It's over." He turned toward her. "Let's make a break for it. Just leave."

"You have no idea how good that sounds right now. I would love to do that, and you know it. But—"

A door opened ahead of them. Parkman stuck his head out and waved for them to hurry. Without debate, they ran the rest of the way and turned into the room, Sarah first.

Parkman had the TV on, tuned to a news station. Sarah heard her name. Then, comments about the prison bus.

Parkman closed and secured the door behind him.

Sarah gawked at the screen. The police were searching for her. If anyone saw her, they were to call the number on the screen. They were instructed not to approach her as she was considered armed and dangerous. The search was province-wide, as she had been seen in Kingston and, most recently, Toronto.

"What the hell is this?" she asked.

Parkman turned off the TV. "You're wanted for questioning regarding the prison bus attack." He tossed the remote onto the bed. "Apparently, you were witnessed at the scene of the accident."

She exchanged a glance with Aaron. "We were there. But we were trying to help."

Aaron shook his head. "We had nothing to do with it. If anything, the fact that we were seen there was my fault. Sarah warned me, but I wanted to help."

She rubbed his arm. "It's okay. No one gets arrested for goodwill."

Parkman raised his eyebrows and tilted his head. "No one? All you ever do is help people, and how many times have you been arrested?"

Deflated, exhausted, Sarah pulled out the chair from the small desk and plopped down. "What do we do?"

"Tell me everything," Parkman said. "Start after we parted ways. No one knows you're here. The room's in my name."

Sarah related their drive out of Toronto, what Vivian said about the prison bus, and how it all happened. She told him about renting a new car using Benjamin's credit card and finished with having Casper pull a police car off their tail by calling him for the favor.

"How did he manage that?" Parkman asked, pointing at

the TV. "After what you just saw. Every cop in the province —probably the country—is looking for you."

"Who knows how Casper does anything," Aaron added.

"Tell us what happened to you today," Sarah said. "What happened to your phone?"

Parkman told them how he had muted his phone and then explained about the man who followed him to the parking garage in terminal three. The man said he was responsible for the bus attack and that he'd killed his brother. Also, that he'd quit the force.

"What the hell?" Aaron whispered. "He was that cop? The one who chased us? No wonder we got away so easily."

Parkman shook his head. "He mentioned the name *Blacken*. He called him *The* Blacken. Not sure why."

Aaron walked over and opened the curtains.

"What next?" Parkman asked.

"I need your help," Sarah said. "One more time."

He nodded. "Anything, Sarah."

Aaron turned from the window and crossed his arms. "This the rest of Vivian's message?"

Sarah nodded. "It is. You won't like it much, but I need you both to listen and do as I say. Any deviance will get me killed."

"For real?" Aaron asked.

"Seriously killed?" Parkman asked. "Like dead?"

Sarah rubbed her face and turned back to the best men in her life. "In the grave, six-feet-deep dead. No coming back kinda dead."

"And if we listen to you—" Parkman started.

"—we can avoid that?" Aaron finished.

"That's what Vivian and I are hoping for. I, for one, want to keep breathing for several more years."

Parkman sat on the edge of the bed. Aaron retreated from the window and dropped beside Parkman. The men looked at each other, then at Sarah.

"Tell us," Aaron said. "We're ready."

Sarah told them what they had to do to keep her alive.

Her prediction was correct: neither man liked it at all.

In fact, they hated it.

Chapter 10

BLACKEN WOKE WITH A splitting headache. But the pain didn't stop there. His wrists hurt, his ankles hurt, and most of all, his jaw hurt.

He moaned, tried to move his tongue, then stopped moving. It was futile. Something clearly blocked his mouth.

A gag.

Consciousness shot to the surface, along with awareness. He'd been about to grab Kym and take her to his car. Make things right.

Something stopped him. But how?

He flitted his eyes, trying to open them, but the light was too bright.

"He's awake, sir." An unfamiliar voice.

"Good." Jensen.

Blacken swiveled as far as his restraints allowed him to follow the voice. It took some of the direct light off his face. He was on the floor in the house's basement and leaning hard on one shoulder. He moved around for comfort.

Squinting, he could see figures in the room about him. The headache forced his eyes closed, but Blacken pushed back, keeping them slightly open. Jensen stood in front of him, arms crossed. Behind Jensen were two rather large men in matching suits. Beyond them, by the door, was his wife, holding a large glass of wine. The small rectangular window above her head and to the right was dark.

How long have I been out?

He lowered his head and tried to move his hands again, a moan escaping his gagged mouth.

"You're not going anywhere," Jensen said, leaning in closer, "after what you did." He shook his head in disgust. "You're not going anywhere for a long time."

Then Jensen grabbed something in front of Blacken's mouth and yanked. The gag pulled out, his mouth involuntarily snapping shut.

He moaned, this time louder. The pain in his jaw made him not want to move his mouth. Having been cranked open for however long must've strained it, not to mention the arid, cotton-mouth feel.

"Get him some water," Jensen said.

One of the men stepped away.

Blacken eased to his other side and rested while he waited for the water. He wasn't beaten. He wasn't finished. He would find a way to escape, take Kym, and leave this place. Forcible confinement, kidnapping, and a host of other charges pending for his boss would make this an easy escape. To use as much force as was necessary—and then some— was a given. But until he broke free, he would appear docile, beaten, defeated.

Jensen moved away to whisper something to Kym. They chatted by another door to the basement, glancing back at him periodically.

He lowered his head to the concrete floor, breathing evenly, slowly. Through the pain, he studied as much of the basement as he could. There was one door to his left and another beside Kym to the far right. Windows weren't really an option as they were tiny rectangles near the ceiling— unless he had something to prop himself up on.

The first step would be getting untied. A bathroom break. To eat. He needed some reason to have his restraints taken off. Then he would pounce. That was the entire plan, which wasn't much of a plan at all. He needed something better. Something more solid. He needed to get out of Jensen's basement with his wife for anything to work out in his favor.

The man returned with the water. His partner stepped forward and pulled Blacken to a sitting position. Once the cup was brought to his lips, it was tilted back slightly. Blacken sipped, filling his mouth with water and wishing several painkillers were going down with it.

A door closed.

Behind the man with the water, Jensen approached. Kymberly was gone. That door was now shut.

"That's enough," Jensen said.

The water was pulled away. The man holding him let go, and Blacken slipped sideways and lightly smacked the concrete floor with his shoulder. Gently, he lowered his head and stared at nothing, the water filling his belly, moistening his lips.

"Why come here?" Jensen asked.

Blacken didn't say a word.

"Who did you hire?" Jensen tried again.

From the corner of his eye, Blacken detected Jensen nodding.

One of the men in suits stepped closer, reared his foot back, and kicked Blacken in the stomach.

He wasn't prepared for the hit. Reflexively, his body curled inward as he fought for a breath, pain exploding everywhere, his headache flaring.

"Again," Jensen shouted.

The man reared back.

"Nooo—" Blacken tried to shout, but nothing came out as the man's foot sank deep in his abdomen.

Sparks flared in his consciousness as the pain grew from intolerable to unmanageable. No amount of breath passed his lips. The wind knocked out of him, he silently gasped for air like a landed fish. If the man kicked him again, he would lose consciousness for sure.

He tightened his jaw, clenched his teeth, and endured the pain.

Jensen touched the man's arm and eased him back.

"Ready to answer questions now?"

Blacken forced himself to look at Jensen as bits of air returned to his lungs. He gave a barely perceptible nod.

"Good." Jensen produced a picture from his inside jacket pocket. He held it in a way that didn't allow his hired men to see it. "Who took this photo?"

Blacken shrugged.

"You don't get it, do you?" Jensen waved an arm behind him. "These men work for a powerful boss in town. They're on loan to me as a favor. After what happened recently to the seven families in Toronto, I've been asked to clean up this mess personally." He folded the photo in half and jammed it in a pocket. "When you interfere, as you did with the bus and with hiring someone to investigate me, you put your future on the line." Jensen got to his feet. "And I'm not talking about your future as a detective. I'm talking about your *future*. As in, you may not have one."

Jensen nodded and stepped away. Both men moved forward. One lowered to his knees in front of Blacken while the other stood near his stomach.

Blacken shook his head. The expression on the closest man's face didn't change. He raised his hand, the fingers curling back into a fist, then slammed it onto Blacken's cheek as the other man's foot rammed into his stomach again.

The world turned black.

Chapter 11

Sarah made it to the hotel room's door and stopped there.

"This is important. We can't miss anything."

"We know," Aaron said. "We'll do as you've asked."

Sarah turned back. "I thought we'd be far from this by now, Aaron. I thought we'd be relaxing by a hotel pool, on vacation by now."

"I did, too."

She glanced at Parkman. "I'm sorry to drag you into this."

"Sarah. Come on. I'm Parkman. Which means I'm always there for you. Forever. This has been my life's work since I met you at Dolan's. That was quite a few years ago, and we're still doing this, still a team."

She looked down at her hands. After a moment, she

glanced up.

"Something feels wrong about this one, though."

Aaron stepped closer. "Wrong, how?"

"Just off. Vivian is off. She won't tell me who betrayed me. She won't tell me how or why that prison bus accident is tied to me. She isn't telling me a thing about what's happening, just what I need to do to prepare for what's coming." She shook her head as if to clear it. "It's like we're to prepare for an unavoidable war. Wouldn't it be easier just to quell the war? Deal with the aggressor on their side?"

"Isn't that what we're doing?" Parkman asked. "Dealing with the aggressor?"

Sarah shrugged, then raised her head and jutted out her chin. "It's fine. We'll deal with this like we've dealt with everything before it." She opened the door and stepped into the hallway. "I guess I just thought it was over for a bit. That Aaron and I could take a break and rediscover each other. Take time for us." She looked into his eyes and felt the longing she saw there.

"In time, Sarah," he whispered and moved closer. "Will you be okay? There are a lot of cops out there, and they're all looking for you."

She pulled her hair together, piled it on her head, and then placed the ball cap Parkman had bought her in the hotel gift shop on top.

"I'll be fine. I just need you guys there on time. I'll likely be unconscious when we see each other again." She looked from Aaron to Parkman, then back to Aaron. "My life will be in your hands, providing I'm not shot the night before."

Aaron shrugged. "Well, sure, there's that."

"Don't get shot," Parkman said. "Easy as that."

"Yeah, sure," Sarah said. "Easy." She let the door close.

Alone in the corridor, she started for the stairs. On the first floor, she exited through the side of the building and walked away from the hotel under the cover of night.

She had a place to be. A small motel ten blocks away was about to be raided by four men. People would be killed in their sleep, money taken. The motel was rumored to be holding men from a rival gang, but it didn't have any gang members there. Just business people and a couple of families from out of town.

Vivian explained it was faulty intel from a man named Blacken. He'd sent the gang unit to the wrong location—intentionally.

Sarah planned on being there with half an hour to spare. Vivian was clear on the directions and what to do to stop it, too.

But most of all, Vivian wanted this act to be heroic. Something the media would print.

The beginning of changing the public's perception of Sarah. Something the authorities enjoyed besmirching at every turn.

After all she'd been through and done for the authorities in the past, if anything were a betrayal, what the police were doing would certainly qualify.

She picked up her pace, not wanting to be late.

It was a life-or-death matter.

Chapter 12

THE SMALL RECTANGULAR WINDOW was still dark when he woke in the basement. He rolled onto his back, grunting with the pain in his abdomen. His cheek flared where he'd been punched. It might have been only one punch, but he got hit twice. Once with the fist and the second time when his face bounced off the concrete floor. He was out by the time he hit the concrete, but its mark was there. He felt it when he winced.

The house was silent above him. It had to be near midnight, maybe later. He wondered if Kym was in bed with Jensen a few floors above him.

What was Jensen's endgame? They'd not liked each other for some time. Still, when he'd suspected Kymberly of infidelity and hired a private investigator to learn more, he had never suspected her lover was Jensen. Which led him to believe Kym was a pawn in Jensen's game, whatever that might be.

Jensen had said the large men were on loan to him. Entrusted to him or something like that. Because Jensen was given the task of cleaning things up. What the hell was he talking about, and how did it relate to what Blacken was doing?

Blacken had no idea Jensen was involved in anything outside work. And maybe that was all it was. They were both actively pursuing outdoor work, and somehow, their paths collided unbeknownst to Blacken.

Blacken would have to un-collide them. Jensen wouldn't kill him. He wasn't a murderer. Either Blacken would escape his bindings, or Jensen would release him in time. Then he'd straighten it all out.

But that was the problem. Blacken didn't have time. He needed out immediately. He'd had Rob Russell take out the prison bus. He'd leaked false information to the gang unit, knowing full well one of their informants would learn of that specific intel and take action. His goal was to spin it with Sarah Roberts involved. Ultimately, he'd reach out to Sarah, getting her cell phone number from a friend on the force.

He was prepared to call her and make a deal. Once they met up, he would offer her an out, and all would be well.

But none of that would happen with him tied up in Jensen's basement in Barrie, an hour's drive from Toronto. For all he knew, Sarah was hightailing it out of town now that every police officer in Ontario had her picture with orders to bring her in. Even overzealous private citizens would be watching for her.

People loved a hero, but when that hero went rogue, they didn't just hate them, they despised them, and right about now, most of Toronto and the surrounding area were probably pretty angry at Sarah, even if those men on the bus were convicted criminals. Decent folk didn't like people who burned others en masse in a bus.

He licked his lips and tested the bonds on his hands. His chafed wrists protested, and he stopped moving. The house creaked above. He listened for more movement but heard nothing.

With all that had happened, he forgot to call in that Russell's debt had been paid. One of the men on that bus had been marked for execution by the Lombardi people. Blacken had brokered a deal for Russell's debt. The Lombardi people would hear about it in the papers, but Blacken had wanted to make the call and seal the deal.

None of that mattered now. He lifted his head and tried his wrists again. They were bound too tight. How the hell did they expect a man to piss? And no one had asked him about a washroom break.

To his right was a small circular grate.

"No way," he muttered to himself.

They'd strategically placed him by a drain so he could piss himself whenever he wanted, knowing full well he'd hold his other business for several days if he had to.

"Bastards."

A door opened. One of the men from earlier stepped in sans jacket. He eased the door closed without making a sound. The man wasn't just tall—he was thick, too. Thick chest, thick arms.

"Thirsty?" he asked.

"Yes." Blacken had wanted to swear at him, cuss him out. He wanted to demand to be released. He was a detective with the Toronto Police Department, for fuck's sake. But none of that would matter if what Jensen said was true. If, in fact, this man was with one of the seven families in Toronto, swearing at him would only get Blacken another boot, but probably in the mouth this time.

The man disappeared through the door. A moment later, he returned with a glass of water. He kneeled close, lifted Blacken's head, and allowed him to drink all of it in one go.

"Thank you."

The man didn't acknowledge him.

"How long am I supposed to be here?"

The man rose to his feet and started for the door.

"You talk?"

"Yes, I talk. But no questions. I answer nothing."

It was the first time Blacken detected a slight accent.

"Italian. I hear it in your voice."

The man stopped at the open door. He turned back slightly, waited a moment like he wanted to say something, then moved away.

"Get Jensen down here. I want to talk."

The door closed without a sound.

"Fuck you," he whispered.

After five more minutes of listening to the house, wondering if the hired help would call Jensen down to chat, he realized no one was coming.

With his limited movement, Blacken eased his hands to

the left to feel if his wallet was still there—it was. A good sign. They probably frisked him but left his personal belongings on him.

He eased his hands to the right and discovered his car keys were still there. Even the keychain.

That was a mistake.

The keychain was a harmless-looking piece of metal, but it wasn't harmless at all. It was a kubaton. He had trained years before in a self-defense class on properly using a kubaton. Held in a fist when punching, the keys would tear skin. Held on someone's wrist, the kubaton would bring an opponent to the floor.

Why the hell would they leave the kubaton in his pocket? Surely, one of those guys knew what it was. Unless they knew Blacken could never access it while tied up.

Or if they felt he would never get the chance to use it because he wouldn't be alive long enough.

A sinking feeling that Jensen was into something so big that Blacken had to be removed came over him. Take Blacken's wife. Then, take his life.

Two goons borrowed for a job.

Two goons from one of the seven families had just taken major hits because of Sarah Roberts.

Maybe something big was happening, and Blacken had gotten in the way. Perhaps he was on the way out.

Blacken wouldn't go down without a fight and couldn't fight in this position.

He rolled into a sitting position and examined the basement for weapons, a way out, or anything to start a fire.

It was time to fight back.

Chapter 13

SARAH SLOWED ON THE sidewalk in front of the small two-story motel. Calling the police wasn't an option. She wished it were that easy. They would arrive with the wrong focus: arrest Sarah Roberts.

It would waste precious time, and people would die.

The police would come eventually, but not until they learned of the crisis.

She waited for a small group of cars to pass, then edged out and made a beeline for the café attached to the motel. The windows were dark, but it looked like someone was still inside. She hoped there was at least a half hour to prepare, but she probably had less.

The motel had a dozen vehicles parked in random areas. Families are on vacation, people are traveling through, and there are a couple of work trucks. All the people had no idea a group of four men were coming with weapons and the intent to kill. Coming on false information from a solid source.

Parkman had said *that the Blacken had plans, and people got hurt when the Blacken had plans.*

The guy who talked to Parkman in the airport parking garage had unsettled him. *Warn Sarah.* Well, Parkman didn't like those words. Add that to what she told him and Aaron to do, and it was a catastrophe. It took every ounce of pleading for them to give in and do it her way—Vivian's way, really.

She tried the café's door. It was locked.

She cupped her face on the glass and peered inside. A woman stood by the counter drying cutlery. She paused to look up at Sarah, shook her head, and mouthed the word, *closed,* then continued drying her forks and spoons with a white towel.

Sarah knocked.

The woman glanced up and shouted, "Closed!" with more frustration, then returned to her work.

Sarah knocked again. She had to get inside the café. Hoping it would still be open had been a long shot. Having an employee still on site was perfect. She needed it to stay closed, though. The woman could go home and avoid the men who were coming.

She knocked again, trying the door hard enough to make it clang against the door frame.

The woman set down her towel and stared at Sarah, an angry expression creasing her pretty features. Sarah shrugged and smiled back.

"I need to talk to you," Sarah shouted through the door.

The woman tilted her head slightly, and then, like an epiphany hit her, the anger dissipated like sand through her fingers, and her face lit up. She half ran, half jogged across the floor, dodging tables and chairs, meandering her way to the entrance, her grin widening as she ran.

At the door, the café woman clicked the thumb latch and opened it.

"Are you Sarah?" the woman asked, holding the door open.

"You know me?"

"Oh my … I can't," the woman placed a hand on her chest and stepped back. "What you've done for so many people over the years, I just can't believe you're here. Is it really you?"

Sarah stepped inside and closed the door behind her. She clicked the lock in place.

The expression on the woman's face soured. "Oh shit. Wait, what's this mean? Is trouble coming my way? Are you here for me?"

Sarah read her nametag, then met her gaze.

"Lacee, trouble is coming, but you'll be okay."

"Oh, thank God. You had me there for a second." She stepped back to take Sarah in. "It's really you."

"Look, Lacee, I'm not a celebrity. I'm just—"

"I know. I get it. It's been many years since those religious freaks were in Toronto killing cops. It's just that your name hits the papers off and on. What were they called again?" Lacee seemed a little flustered, her hand still on her chest.

"The Rapturites."

"Right." Lacee snapped her fingers. "Those guys. Bastards. Then the street gangs and so many other things you've dealt with."

Sarah walked past her toward the kitchen. "I'm never comfortable meeting someone who knows so much about me."

"Get used to it," Lacee said from behind her as she followed close. "The media loves someone like you."

"It's not mutual, I assure you."

"You're an inspiration, Sarah."

She turned back at the kitchen door. "How so?"

"You've inspired me over the years. I left an abusive man. You gave me strength. I'm stronger as a woman than ever before. Watching you deal with all that shit, and I don't know the half of it, just what the papers have told me off and on over the years. But knowing you're out there, well, you inspired me to fix my life. If you could fight cops and the Italian mob and everyone else, then I could at least leave an abusive man and take my son with me."

Time was running out, but something about this woman made Sarah pause. An inner strength, a vitality. She held out a hand. Lacee took it.

"Well then, I'm pleased to meet you. I'm Sarah Roberts."

"It's an honor to meet you. I'm Lacee Faust."

They shook, and then their hands fell away.

"Now, will you help me with weapons?"

"Weapons?" Lacee frowned.

Sarah continued into the kitchen. Lacee followed.

"Yes, weapons. A group of four men will be here shortly.

They have a score to settle and believe their enemies are hiding in this motel."

"What? Oh shit." Lacee braced herself with a hand on the counter. "Okay, I'll call the police."

"Don't," Sarah snapped. "They'll arrest me and leave. People in this motel will be killed."

"I saw that bus thing on the news. What the hell? I mean, you wouldn't randomly kill people, even if they were prisoners. The cops obviously don't know you." She paused. "Right?"

Sarah glanced at her, then kept searching drawers. "Right. I've killed before, but I need a reason." Sarah opened another drawer, pulled out a long knife, set it on the counter, and then opened more drawers. "You wouldn't happen to have a gun, would you? I might have to kill someone tonight, and I wouldn't want to bring a knife to a gunfight."

Chapter 14

He was tethered to the wall. There was no way for him to move more than five feet to the left or right. His hands and ankles were bound, and his face was swollen.

Angry and despondent, he waited for someone to return and was rewarded when Jensen entered the basement.

Jensen held a glass of red wine and wore a T-shirt and track pants.

"Relaxing with my wife?" Blacken asked.

"She's not your wife anymore."

"Fuck you, Jensen. She can say whatever she wants, but she's my wife. I have papers to prove that."

"You're considered legally separated." He sipped from his glass from about ten feet away. "So fuck you back."

"This is high school now?"

"You know you're dead, right?"

Blacken took in a deep breath, then exhaled. "Interesting. I'm still breathing, asshole."

"You've fucked with the wrong people."

"Oh yeah. Who's that?"

Jensen took another drink, his eyes never leaving Blacken. "They'll be here tomorrow. They want a chat with you."

"I can't have a sit down shackled like this."

"You won't be getting out of those restraints, Blacken. Not in this life. You'll die in them down here."

"And you're okay with that? Murder in your basement?"

"It's out of my hands." He sipped his wine again like he was hurrying to get drunk. "You made this bed. You're dead, regardless. My contribution only propels my career."

"Fuck you, Jensen. Other things are at play here."

"Like what?" Jensen shrugged as if Blacken's words didn't bother him, but Blacken detected a hint of nervousness.

He diverted his gaze. They were talking in circles. Jensen had the upper hand, and he knew it. Any tough talk from Blacken would appear as desperation. There was no use. He would have to wait until he figured a way out.

Gang unit officers? Pissed about his misleading their investigation? More men from the seven families tied to the two brutes in the other room? Why would the Toronto mafia have an interest in Blacken? How could he have gotten on their radar?

He laughed under his breath at how fucked everything was.

"What's so funny?" Jensen asked.

When Blacken looked back at him, the wine was half gone. Jensen's eyes had that glazed look of a little too much wine.

"You're drunk."

"No, I'm not."

"Are you nervous, Jensen? About what's coming?"

"Nervous?" He clucked his tongue. "Absolutely not."

"Then what's going on, Jensen? You can tell me. We go way back."

Jensen shrugged and turned back to the open door, where he stopped and stared at Blacken.

"I know what's coming, and I couldn't care less. One more asshole rogue cop is dead. I'll report you as missing in the line of duty. Kym gets the pension. We're all good."

"Then why are you nervous?"

Jensen drained his wine glass and lowered his hand to the side, holding the glass by the stem. A couple of drips escaped the rim and hit the concrete floor.

"I'm nervous because I suspect they'll want me to pull the trigger."

That hit Blacken in the gut. People were coming to kill him. For what, he still didn't know. But making Jensen do it after Jensen stole his wife and fucked him over.

"That would suck, eh Jensen?"

"Make no mistake, I would kill you now if those men weren't coming with their questions tomorrow. You're a piece of shit, and you're in the way of bigger things. What I don't like is Kym's supposed to witness it. That has the potential to sour our relationship. If that happens, I'll miss out on nailing down your pension, too. You know we're getting married as soon as she's a widow?"

"Fuck you, Jensen." A tear threatened to escape. He couldn't let Jensen see him cry. "I'll kill you myself, Jensen. Release me, and let's fight it out."

"I'm not that stupid. I'd rather you die tied up. Easier that way."

Blacken shifted position and rolled toward Jensen, a grunt escaping his lips. The chain linking him to the wall snapped taut.

"I'll kill you," he shouted. "I'll fucking kill you."

"Goodnight, Blacken."

The door closed. Another one opened. One of the men stepped into the room. He glanced left toward the other door, then over to Blacken. After a moment, he stepped back inside his room and closed the door.

Blacken was alone. Those tears escaped.

His bladder had held on long enough.

A stream of urine released, soaking his pants and pooling below him. Then, it headed toward the drain.

He curled into a ball as best he could and wept.

Chapter 15

ARAH FIDGETED, WAITING FOR an answer.

"I don't have a gun in my café," Lacee said. "But I've got this." She pulled out a small cylindrical device. "Bear spray." She handed it to Sarah. "Like pepper spray or Mace. Will it help?"

"Yes. It'll help. How about a small knife? A small, sharp knife."

"Here." Lacee pulled on a cabinet door, slid out another drawer, and produced a selection of paring knives. "Take any you want."

"Then I need you to leave," Sarah said.

"Leave? What do you mean?"

Sarah stopped, a paring knife in her hand. "The men coming here tonight think the people they're looking for are hiding in the rooms of this motel. Once they learn that's untrue, they'll come to this café. You don't want to be here when that happens."

Lacee held Sarah's gaze for a moment, then looked away. "Okay, I can leave."

Sarah grabbed three small knives, slipped one in each back pocket, kept one in her hand, and placed the bear spray in her front pocket. She snatched up a couple of white dinner plates and headed for the door that led directly into the motel.

"Promise me you'll go home now," Sarah said.

Lacee followed her to the door. "I promise. Once you're inside the motel, I'll lock this door, head out the employee entrance at the back, and drive home."

"Thank you. Hear all about what happened tomorrow. Come to work as if nothing has changed." Sarah turned back to face Lacee. "You know nothing and didn't see me. That cool?"

Lacee smiled. It brightened her face. "Very cool. If it'll help you, Sarah, I'd gladly do it. I'll be in my minivan and out of here in under two minutes."

"Good. And Lacee?"

"Yeah?"

"Thanks. Really. I mean that."

Lacee moved forward. They embraced. After a moment, they released.

"The thanks goes to you, Sarah."

She nodded at Lacee, backed out the door, and started for the lobby. The door locked behind her.

Good. One less person on site.

At the counter, the clerk was setting the phone down. She

smiled wide as Sarah approached.

"How can I help you?"

Sarah read her nametag. "Janet, I need your help with something."

"Do you have a room here?"

"No, but I want—"

"Are you looking to check in or make a reservation?"

"Janet, I'm—"

"Janet Kirsten is my name. It's late, and I'm tired. My evening relief didn't show. Shift change was at eleven. So, if you don't have a room and aren't interested in one, I'm unsure how I could help you. I need to get back on the phone to hunt down a relief."

The nice approach wasn't working.

"Janet Kirsten, I need you to tell me how many people are staying in your motel tonight, and I need a list of room numbers. I need this as fast as possible."

"I'm sorry, you must be mistaking me for someone else." She placed a hand on the top of the desk. "This is the front desk of a motel, and I'm the clerk. We don't give out that kind of information. Please leave, or I'll have to call security."

"You don't have security here. I checked. If there's an issue, you have a security company you can call to evict a room, but by the time they get here, I'll have the information I need."

"Oh no, you won't, missy." Janet picked up the phone and smacked the numbers. "Why would you want to know how many people are in this motel, anyway?"

"So I know how many people will die in five to ten

minutes because you didn't give me the information I needed."

"I'm calling the police."

Chapter 16

BLACKEN HAD DRIFTED OFF to sleep, his pants cold with urine. But it couldn't have been more than a few minutes before something clicked nearby, startling him awake.

Kymberly leaned against the basement wall, arms crossed, watching him, her expression shrouded in shadow.

"What do you want?" he asked. "To posture and revel in seeing me tied up in Jensen's basement?"

She wiped her cheek. Was she crying?

"I came down because I …"

"What? You what?"

She cleared her throat. "Because I wanted to say I was sorry."

"Bit late for that now."

She pushed off the wall and moved toward him. "What

were you going to do when you saw me earlier? When you rushed me? Before Jensen's security knocked you out?"

"They were waiting in that room behind me, weren't they?"

She nodded. "They'd seen you on camera watching the house from beyond the fence in the back. They tracked your every step."

"Were you really on the phone, then?"

She shook her head. "A ruse to bring you to the third floor."

"Why the third floor? I'm tied up in the basement."

"Like a guard tower in a prison, these guys like elevated positions to monitor the grounds. When they saw you," she shrugged, "they just wanted you up here."

"Monitor the grounds? This house is in a residential area. There are no grounds."

"Look, I don't know these guys or their routine. It was just what I was told. They're on loan for a few days."

He swallowed. That confirmed a lot of what Jensen had said. Mortality was something to think about. He may have less than twelve hours to live, and he still had no idea why.

"You know Jensen's plan?"

She nodded.

"And you're okay with it?"

She didn't nod this time, but her eyes didn't leave him. Those same eyes he fell in love with long ago. His high school date to the prom. He'd fallen for Kymberly when everyone went for Apryl, her sister. He'd asked her out several times, but it wasn't until the prom that she said she'd go as his date. They hung out that summer, and they were dating by the next year when college started. Then married and now heading to divorce, or in his case, until death did they part.

"I overheard him talking to you," she said. She wiped her face again. "I didn't know all that. Jensen lied to me."

"Lied." Blacken let out a short laugh. "I've never trusted Jensen. You, of all people, know that. How many times have we talked about him and his fucking around on the job with countless women? How many times has he been suspected of concealing evidence? But then *he* gets promoted." Blacken shook his head. "I just thought you knew better."

"He said the same about you. Then I heard you'd hired someone to follow me. You wanted pictures, Joey, so we gave you pictures."

That hurt. Seeing her with Jensen dug his heart out. Made him crazy. Made him murderous.

"My name is Joel. You know I don't like when you call me Joey."

"You liked it when we were first dating."

"I liked everything when we were first dating." He waited a heartbeat. "So, what did he tell you about this, this kidnapping of a detective and murder scheme of his?"

"That you were being held here until tomorrow. After that, you would be transported back to Toronto for processing for several offenses relating to breaking into his house and attacking me."

"Why not do that earlier? Why wait until tomorrow? You know as well as I do suspects are processed immediately. They aren't held overnight in someone's basement, guarded by mafia henchmen."

"Jensen said the police were taxed at the moment. Something about that girl, Sarah Roberts. And he said there was some kind of gang war happening in town. The Emergency Task Force was on standby."

"And you believed him?"

She nodded and moved closer. Something was in her hand, but she wasn't close enough for him to see it.

"You don't think officers stay in the police station to process suspects all day long, regardless of emergencies?"

"Of course, Joey. I know they do. I just thought you were a high-profile situation, and he'd rather deal with you tomorrow."

He decided to let the use of his nickname go this time. "And now you've heard what dealing with me tomorrow means, right?"

She nodded, then moved even closer, her hand still hidden in shadow.

"What you got there?" he asked.

She glanced at the door the two goons used, then back at him.

"I will tell you a few things, then leave." Her voice was soft, quiet. Evidently, she didn't want the two goons to interrupt them.

He nodded for her to go ahead.

She eased closer, kneeling a couple of feet from him.

"I have fallen out of love with you, Joel." She held up a hand. "Don't protest or say anything. Let me have my piece."

He nodded, glanced down at the concrete floor, then back to her.

"Go ahead," he whispered. "I'm listening."

"I fell out of love a long time ago. I'm unhappy, Joel. Jensen changed that for me. That's all this is."

He didn't respond. Just stared at her, waiting for her to continue.

She wiped her other cheek and looked down at her hands. He was able to see what she carried now.

A set of keys.

"The truth?" Her head shot up, and she stared into his eyes. "I grew to hate you and don't care if you're arrested, imprisoned, destitute, or begging on the street. Or if you make it big and become a wealthy guy. Frankly, I just don't care anymore."

"So then, why are you here? Trying to cheer me up?"

"I may hate you, Joel, and I may want terrible things to happen because of the emotional abuse you've made me suffer, but I don't wish you dead. I've never wished you dead."

"Great. So only Jensen wants me dead."

"Yeah, and that's not going to happen—as much as I'd love the pension. After what he just said, I'll have to rethink my position with him."

Hope sprung in his gut, sending a warmth through his abdomen.

"So, what are you saying, Kym?"

She held out the keys. "These will release you. But you have to promise to leave out the back. As soon as you trigger the motion detector lights, you'll be on camera, and these guys will pursue, so run fast."

"I can do that."

"Promise me you won't run to the Barrie Police

Department and do anything stupid. Jensen has a lot of powerful friends. They met here a couple of times. I've stayed out of the way, but I recognized faces. Just promise me you'll run. Go home. Gather other cops around you. Find out why you're a target."

He offered her a calm expression. "I'm sorry it came to this, and I'm sorry I wasn't a better husband—"

"Bullshit."

"Let me finish. I truly want to say this as it'll probably be our last time alone. I am sorry for all of that. I still remember the girl I took to the prom in high school."

She fiddled with the keys, obviously uncomfortable with what he was saying.

"Be careful, Kym. Do what's right for you. Knowing what you did for me here, I'll remember it going forward. When we're in divorce court, I'll be fair. In fact, you'd be the reason I'm still alive, so I'll be more than fair."

"Joel, you don't have to secure your release by negotiating with me. Regardless of what you might bargain, I'm letting you go because I won't have your death on my conscience, and I was lied to about what would happen to you."

They'd said enough. It was time to make a break for it.

"Then let's do this," he whispered. "Before gorilla one or gorilla two come out and stop you."

She edged closer, careful to stay out of the urine spot on the concrete. After fiddling with two keys, she located the right one and undid his ankles first. He moved his feet around to increase circulation as she worked on freeing his hands.

The key slid inside. She waited a moment, then looked

up at him.

"No funny stuff, right?" she asked.

"No funny stuff."

"You won't attack me as soon as you're free?"

He frowned. "You serious? After you saved my life? I have *some* gratitude." He acted affronted. "And honor," he added.

She turned the key. "Don't kid yourself, Joey. You have no honor. But I've seen gratitude in the past."

The manacles came off his wrists. He sat up as she handed him the keys and got to her feet.

"I'll tell Jensen that I dropped the keys, and you were able to snatch them up before I could retrieve them."

"Why would you have the keys out in the first place?" he asked.

"To taunt you."

He nodded. "That works. He'll believe that."

She pointed at a door on the other side of the basement. "Leave through that door. As soon as it opens, I'll run upstairs shouting for Jensen. He's asleep in a wine coma."

"We have a deal," Blacken said, getting to his feet stiffly. He did several stretches to loosen cramped muscles. "One hug goodbye?"

She glanced down at his wet pants, then back to his face. "Don't touch me with that. I don't want your pee on me."

"This is a goodbye hug in honor of our years together."

She leaned in, her pelvis extended away. "You have no honor, Joey."

He wrapped his arms around her shoulders and held on for a moment. When she made to pull away, he released her, reared back, and sucker-punched her with as much force as he could muster in one blow.

Without a sound, her eyes rolled back in her head as her legs crumpled awkwardly under her. She fell hard, but the concrete floor swallowed most of the impact.

"You're right, bitch. I have no honor." He massaged his hand. "And don't call me Joey."

He moved to the door where the goons were and knocked. Then he yanked out his kubaton.

Payback time.

Chapter 17

SARAH WATCHED JANET KIRSTEN as she stopped dialing the phone, her hands visibly shaking. "Why are people going to die in this motel?" she asked.

There was no time for talking. The men would be there at any moment.

"I'm Sarah Roberts. Look me up in your spare time—"

"I know who you are. Your face has been all over the news today."

"Fine. Now that we know each other, Janet, you may also know that I often get information about a future event, and I try to stop that bad thing from happening. You're impeding my ability to save lives. So, without further delay, either give me the guests' room numbers quickly, or I will come around the counter and get them myself."

Janet's mouth opened at Sarah's bold approach. She'd probably never had anyone speak to her in such a way.

Sarah didn't wait. She hopped up onto the counter and launched over it, landing solidly on her feet.

"What are you doing—" Janet nearly shrieked.

"Shut the fuck up." Not only was she out of time, but she'd also lost patience with Janet as well.

She tapped on the computer screen on her side of the desk. A password window came up.

"Give me the password."

Janet had moved away, heading for the staff exit that would bring her out into the main lobby.

"You're in a lot of trouble," Janet stammered. "The police are on their way—"

"What?"

Desperate, Sarah gawked at the TV display to her left. Eight cameras covered the grounds. One near the restaurant's front door, one in the lobby, and six others inside and outside the building.

Sarah put it together in seconds.

"You saw me enter the café, didn't you? You saw my face on the news today." She glared at Janet. "When I came in here, you were on the phone, but it had nothing to do with finding a replacement for a no-show on your shift. You called the police, didn't you?"

Janet was by the front doors now. She gripped the horizontal bar, nodding back at Sarah. "They'll be here any minute."

"You've done a terrible thing, Janet."

Movement caught her eye on the camera. She bent to get

a closer look. Two men in balaclavas slipped by a camera positioned in spot three.

She shot up and gawked at Janet. "Where's camera three pointing?"

Janet shrugged, defiant to the end.

"Fuck," she blurted out.

Someone ran by the door behind Janet.

He also wore a balaclava.

"Get away from the door," she said in a hushed tone as she ran for the employee exit.

"Why, so you can block police access when they get here —"

Glass broke behind her in a shattering cascade. Janet ducked at the sound and dropped to a knee.

Sarah hit the light switch behind the counter as she exited the front desk.

She was no further ahead with learning where guests were staying. Everyone in the motel was at risk now.

The lobby dropped into relative darkness. Outside streetlights and emergency lighting provided enough to move around, but that was it.

"Get down," Sarah whispered, but she didn't have to.

Janet was on her hands and knees, crawling back toward the desk.

"Get out the back door." Sarah ran for the nearest hallway. "Take off your nametag. Do not let these guys think you work here."

She retrieved the bear spray and yanked one of the paring knives out, then shoved her back against a door and entered a stairwell, leaving Janet behind.

"You couldn't have given me more time to prepare, Vivian?" she muttered to herself.

Taking two steps at a time, Sarah jumped onto the second floor and peeked through the rectangular window in the door.

The floor was empty.

If anyone died tonight, it was on the heads of the police. They had been blasting Sarah's image all over the news. Because of them and their fake news, Janet resisted Sarah's requests and even called the authorities on her.

The Toronto Police Department was responsible. One fuck up leads to another.

She opened the door with her left hand, the one holding the paring knife, and kicked the first motel room door she came to, Room 201.

"Open up," she shouted. "Police."

There was no response on the other side of the door. She ran to the next one and kicked the door. "Open up."

No response.

A lock clicked a couple of doors away. A door eased open.

Sarah ran forward as a head popped out.

"What's going on?" a man asked. "I have kids sleeping in here."

"Get them out. Now."

The look on Sarah's face must've startled the man. His head popped back inside, but he left the door open. She stopped in front of it.

The man was grabbing his kids, one in each arm. A woman exited the bathroom, a robe on, brushing her teeth.

"Get out," Sarah said. "The place is being robbed." It

was the best she had, but according to Vivian, the four men in balaclavas were there to silence an enemy who wasn't present. They were ordered to kill anyone in the hotel who stood in their way of searching each and every room. In other words, silence any witnesses.

The woman shrugged and pulled out the toothbrush. "Just lock the door then," she said.

"Not good enough."

She was surprised the men hadn't yet reached the second floor. And she'd only made it to one room.

A weapon was fired somewhere in the building.

"What was that?" the man asked.

"The robbers," Sarah said. "Probably just murdered an entire family," she added for effect.

She stepped back into the hallway, searched the walls, and found what she was looking for.

A red wall-mounted fire alarm.

She jumped to it and yanked it, setting off the blast of noise. It would lead to chaos. People would leave their rooms. The fire department would be called. Emergency services were en route.

She hoped this would end as fast as it started—and without the loss of a single life.

At the family's door, she pushed the dad back inside. "Stay here," she shouted to be heard over the blaring fire alarm. "Lock your family in the bathroom. They won't have time to get up here before the authorities." She moved toward the door when the father nodded. "Lock this behind me."

He nodded again, then set his kids down, a boy and a small girl, no more than three years old, her sleepy face framed by hands over her ears, tears already forming in her eyes.

She stepped back into the corridor, chastising herself for not thinking of the fire alarm earlier.

Two doors had opened at the other end. A man in his fifties or sixties stood outside his door, waiting for someone inside. A woman appeared, and they started along the corridor toward the stairwell on the other side.

Sarah ran for the nearest stairs, saw no one around, and then shoved the door open.

Halfway through the door, someone pushed her hard enough to knock her off her feet.

She body-checked the wall and slumped to the ground, surprised she still held the bear spray. When she spun around and tried to get up, the man was on her, knocking the paring knife from her grasp.

With surprising strength, he held her down and brought his balaclava-covered face to hers, a large gun to her throat.

"Was it you, bitch? You pulled the fire alarm?"

She kicked out with her foot but missed his ankle by inches. Defiantly, she glared into his eyes.

"Fucking coward. Take off the mask." She spit in his face, making him blink. "You're a dead man."

Something on the gun clicked under her chin.

Safety off.

Chapter 18

THE BASEMENT DOOR OPENED.

Blacken was in position, crouched beside it, waiting for the man to move into the basement.

The goon gasped at the site of Kym sprawled out, unconscious beside Blacken's empty restraints.

The man stepped out. Blacken had the kubaton ready, the business end protruding from his fist. He drove it upward, hard and fast, using his legs to push up from his squatted position. The kubaton, along with his fist, connected with the goon's crotch, lifting him off the concrete floor several inches and crushing something in the man's privates.

The man whimpered like a dog, his pitch high, the sound deep inside his throat.

When Blacken pulled his fist away, the goon crumpled to

the floor, hands covering his crotch, curling into a ball, a mask of pain on his face. Before the man could respond, Blacken stood and raised one dress-shoe-covered foot to crash down on the goon's face.

At the last moment, the man tried to jerk out of the way despite the overwhelming pain in his crotch, but he was too late. The heel of Blacken's shoe landed on the man's cheek, crushing his face between Blacken's foot and the unforgiving concrete floor.

Like my sucker punch, asshole, he thought.

Stunned, the man rolled to the side and tried to get to his feet, shaking his head to clear it. Blacken stomped again, a crushing blow to the man's head each time.

"I'm a fucking"—stomp—"officer of the law"—stomp—"asshole." Stomp.

Exhausted, Blacken placed his hands on his thighs and bent at the knees, trying to catch his breath. The goon's face was ruined. Blood covered his head, and the nose twisted in a broken pretzel sort of way. Unconscious wheezing came and went through the man's open mouth. Small pieces of teeth were scattered on the concrete near his open lips, and his jaw protruded upward at an odd angle near where it met his left ear.

Blacken saw the damage and knew it would take months for this man to consider chewing again, and he didn't care one iota. In fact, he felt an insatiable urge to step on the man's face several more times, then hop on his throat, but refrained. There was an escape with death, a way out—he wasn't prepared to give that to these men. The goon living for a year, his jaw wired shut, sipping from a straw, elated

Blacken.

"You wanna fuck with me, you'll fucking pay."

He rifled through the man's pockets and inner jacket. He retrieved a Glock, fully loaded, a billfold with several hundred, and a picture of his whore.

Blacken was sure he'd seen that same girl dancing at the Rushmore Strip Club on the Queensway down in Etobicoke. The club was always being raided for sex and drugs in the VIP room—until recently, when it was rumored to have changed hands. The Lombardi people were said to be the new owners. A classier place that still allowed anything to happen, minus the raids.

It was late. He had assumed they would take shifts. One goon would sleep while the other watched the prisoner. Having seen only this man since dark, he was pretty sure the other man was asleep.

He slipped the cash in one pocket and jammed the Glock in the back of his pants, then hustled back to his unconscious wife and slapped the manacles on her wrists, checking that the tether was still firmly connected to the wall. She wasn't going anywhere unless she wanted to walk in circles for hours. He didn't want to secure her ankles. When they left Jensen's house, he needed her to walk under her own steam. Besides, the ankle manacles would fit nicely on the goon.

He carried them back to the unconscious muscle and clamped them on his ankles with ease. With his face a mess, Blacken didn't think he'd wake up anytime soon. But when he did, he wouldn't be chasing Blacken. He'd be in search of a hospital—where Lombardi's people would find him and, since he fucked up big time, would probably finish Blacken's job for him.

The goon and the wife tied up, he yanked out the Glock, aimed it at the roof, and cleared the room the goon had been in.

Empty.

The other asshole, if he was still inside the house, which Blacken suspected he was, was probably in that third-floor security room Kym had spoken of, where cameras and motion detectors watched the grounds.

Blacken would clear the house alone, quietly. Then he would locate Jensen in his wine coma and remind him why you don't take another man's wife.

"Jensen, I'm coming for you."

He started up the stairs slowly, one at a time, the gun out front.

Chapter 19

Sarah fought back, struggling under the threat of being shot, when Vivian popped into her head.

Stop fighting! her sister shouted. *Think, then fight.*

It startled Sarah into ceasing all movement and going limp. The man's desperate eyes calmed a moment, and he eased the gun back in place.

The fire alarm's shrill sound stopped suddenly, leaving a ringing in her ears.

"Was someone tipped off?" he shouted at her. "How did you know to shut off the lobby's lights? Then pull the alarm?"

A weapon fired somewhere below them again.

Sarah pushed up the wall until she was standing. As she rose, his weapon came up with her, edging closer to her face.

The barrel was an inch from her nose when she was fully standing.

"Are you killing people down there?" she asked, thoroughly disgusted. This was Toronto, not a war zone. Gangs like this were not needed, only bound by a sense of loyalty and the fact that the individual was weak, but in a group, they were tough.

"You think you're a big man because you have your little friends?" She moved forward until her chin touched the tip of the weapon. "Without them, you're nothing."

With the speed Aaron had taught her, she jerked her face to the right, lowered her center of balance, and raised her hands to snap the gun from the man's grasp, all in the same fluid motion. One second, he was holding the gun. The next, Sarah held his gun, and his fingers stung from having had it ripped clear.

He responded by rushing her, grappling for the weapon. She dodged his approach, anticipating it, weaved low and to the right, and slipped by him.

The man in the balaclava fell into the wall.

She trained the weapon on him.

He turned around to face her, his body language proud, chest out, chin pointed upward.

"Mask off," she said.

He didn't move.

She shot him in the shoulder.

The man jerked back with the impact, smacking into the wall. He covered the bullet hole with his free hand and gaped at her.

"You shot me—"

She pulled the trigger again, applying the right amount of pressure at such a close distance that missing the man was nearly impossible. The second bullet jerked the man's arm back as it entered his forearm.

"Mask," she shouted. "Off."

He slowly slipped down the wall, leaving a trail of blood.

Another weapon was fired in the building.

Emergency vehicle sirens wailed in the distance. It was the first she heard them. She needed out. There was no way the police could take her.

Without thinking, acting on instinct alone, she lunged forward, snatched the balaclava, pulled it off the man, and then tossed it down the stairs.

A young man in his early twenties, Hispanic.

"You're out of the crime life, asshole." She aimed the weapon at his foot. "And don't follow me." She fired again.

He screamed in pain as she took the stairs two at a time, heading toward the first floor and three other shooters.

The cops wouldn't be there for a precious minute, and more people could die in that time.

Chapter 20

BLACKEN MADE IT TO the second floor of the large house without incident. The house was quiet. Jensen was probably fast asleep upstairs, and the two occupants downstairs were knocked out.

Only the second goon could potentially be an issue, and Blacken didn't expect to meet up with him until the top floor. But the third floor was shrouded in darkness. It was so black halfway up the stairs that he couldn't see if someone was standing there or not, but he couldn't risk turning on a light.

He pointed the Glock straight ahead and edged up the remaining stairs. Once in the exact same spot where he heard the thump behind him while listening to Kym on her fake call earlier that day, he took a couple of deep breaths to collect his nerves. Adrenaline made him shaky and caused a slightly painful discomfort at the small of his back. A slightly painful reminder of his age. He shifted his hips to break it up, rubbing his lower back to get things circulating.

The door to the master bedroom was open. Just like before, he looked inside. The moonlight through the open window revealed a nicely made-up room. The bed, end tables, and dresser seemed untouched.

He entered the room, slipped across the carpet, and opened the closet door. Just a closet, not a security booth of any sort.

He performed a full circle. The moonlight inside the en suite left no doubt this room was just a room and nothing more.

He entered the corridor again, his heart racing. He rubbed his lower back with a free hand, the Glock hand sweating on the grip.

Where the hell is the other asshole?

He started toward the bedroom Kym had been in when he first broke into the house. The door was slightly ajar. He eased it open without a sound and saw the second goon on the bed, asleep.

Of course. This was their room. The likelihood of attacks would come from the front of the house, where Kym would've felt safe making her fake call. One goon would've stayed with her while the other waited in the master bedroom for Blacken.

He needed to get out of the house, and he needed Kym to go with him. With no time to beat on the second guard, he grabbed a pillow, placed it over his gun hand, and lowered it to the man's face. Once it was on him, he applied pressure to the weapon's trigger.

The man flinched in his sleep, probably detecting the pillow's presence, then jerked awake.

Blacken fired, the sound muffled quite well.

The man's body jerked and spasmed on the bed as Blacken pulled the pillow away. Blood soaked the underside of the pillow. He tossed it in the corner and watched the man for all of two seconds.

Then he left the room as the man's body relaxed in either unconsciousness or death.

Now Jensen.

Where would he sleep?

After a thorough search of the top floor, he couldn't find him. The urge to leave Jensen's house was intense. He still needed to gather Kym and make her walk to his car. But he couldn't leave Jensen sleeping. The man had to pay for what he'd done to Blacken.

On the second floor, a hallway he hadn't seen before led to what Blacken thought was the garage door. He didn't want to leave anywhere without searching it, so he continued, gun at the ready. He passed a laundry room, then stopped at the door to listen.

Nothing.

He turned the knob. It was unlocked and opened easily onto the garage, which was empty.

Empty?

Wouldn't Jensen have parked his vehicle in there?

Blacken eased the door closed. Then he hustled back down the hall to the front window and checked the driveway.

Empty.

Where was Jensen's vehicle? Kymberly's vehicle?

He headed for the kitchen. Jensen had to be in the house. If he didn't find him soon, he'd be forced to head back up to the room where he shot the goon a few minutes before and check the security apparatus. It was probably password-protected and difficult to navigate. But what other options did he have?

Two empty wine bottles sat on the kitchen counter. Beside them were leftover seafood trays, a shrimp bowl, and dip. It reminded Blacken of how hungry he was.

But he ignored it. There would be plenty of time to get food later. Jensen was a top priority.

A note tacked to the fridge caught his attention.

JOEL BLACKEN was written on top in big, block letters.

He lowered the Glock and read the note, his anger rising in his throat to rage. Jensen wrote how he knew Kym had been listening. Jensen knew she had the keys and that she'd free him.

He'd let it all happen because the goons would then punish both of them.

But if Blacken was reading the note, that meant he made it out of the basement. Jensen added on the note that he hadn't drank an ounce of alcohol all night. Carefully designed food coloring and pouring wine down the sink allowed him to take a couple of sips, smell like wine, and even look like he was drinking it, refilling his glass over and over without any effects whatsoever.

Kym had no idea.

Jensen had finished the note while listening to Kym

explain why she set him loose, so Jensen didn't figure Kym would ever reach the kitchen to read it.

Jensen was long gone, and the police had been notified that Blacken had broken in.

He heard a siren in the distance.

"Fuck," he shouted as he slipped the note in his pocket.

If the authorities found him in the house, holding the Glock, and those two goons injured, he wouldn't see this side of prison for a long time. And cops never do well in prison.

He shoved away the Glock as he ran down the stairs toward his unconscious wife. He wouldn't leave without her.

Once everything was over, he would kill Jensen.

There was no other way.

Chapter 21

SARAH REACHED THE FIRST floor without incident, ran to the door that led to the hallway where the rooms were, and yanked it open.

A man several feet from the door spun toward her. Then he took a step her way, raising his weapon.

She fired before he could get his bearings.

The bullet punched a hole in his balaclava by his cheek, knocking him sideways into the wall. He slid down slowly, small twitches in his hands, his arms.

She waited a moment, holding the access door open.

The sirens drew closer.

A door closed somewhere ahead. A man shouted something unintelligible.

Footsteps pounded from inside the room to her right. She

raised her weapon and waited, finger tense on the trigger.

A man in a T-shirt and underwear bounded into the hallway.

A weapon fired inside the room.

Sarah released the tension in her finger and eased it off the trigger, thinking for a split second that she had fired accidentally.

The man smacked into the wall opposite the door and dropped to the carpet. To her relief, he scrambled to his hands and feet, half crawled, half walked a couple of paces, and then ran the length of the hallway to the exit at the end.

Sarah raised her weapon again and waited for the shooter inside the room. She held her breath, eyeing the tip of her weapon, aimed at the shoulder area of an average male height.

"Juan," someone shouted. "Come in here."

The sirens stopped out front.

What is that idiot thinking? The cops are here.

"Hey, Juan."

The speaker wasn't afraid of the police. That part was evident. But why? What was their endgame? A shootout? Death by cop?

"Juan?" the voice was closer to the corridor, closer to Sarah.

Juan didn't answer. Juan lay at Sarah's feet, a bullet hole in his cheek.

She lowered to her knees to make less of a target. The man would be more cautious now. He would wonder why Juan wasn't responding.

"Come out with your hands up!" someone outside the

motel shouted through a bullhorn.

Sarah waited. There had been four of them. She'd dealt with two. The man calling for Juan was number three. Where was number four?

She lowered herself even farther, now sitting on her heels, her shoulder leaning into the wall for balance and stability.

Vivian, what the hell? Help me out of this.

"Fuck it, man," the guy inside the room muttered loud enough for Sarah to hear. He sounded defeated. Something clanged. A door slid open, the sounds of the outside growing louder.

He was leaving the room and heading outside.

"Keep your hands where I can see them," the officer on the bullhorn shouted.

She lowered her arms, exhaled, and slumped on the carpeted motel floor.

Now what?

Allowing them to take her wouldn't work. Not yet. But how could she escape a motel surrounded by cops?

She got to her feet, eased into the darkened lobby, crossed it, and tried the interior door to the café. It was locked.

"Access key is on the table."

Sarah spun at the voice, the gun coming up fast. Janet Kirsten was curled in a corner behind a large fake fern. She put her hands up to ward off a bullet.

Sarah lowered the weapon and moved toward the counter for the access key.

"Sorry, Sarah." Janet was crying. "I didn't know."

"Well, now you do."

"I heard gunfire."

"Those men came to kill everyone in this motel. Many survived." She strode to the café door and stopped. "Calling the police was smart." She looked over her shoulder. "They're outside now, arresting one of them. Don't beat yourself up. You did what anyone else in your shoes would do."

"Thanks for that, but it doesn't feel like it. I should've listened to you."

"Yeah, you should've listened to me."

Sarah inserted the card. The door clicked. She pulled on it and stepped inside the closed café, then paused.

"Hey, Janet?"

"Yeah."

"Do me a favor?"

"I owe you my life."

"Don't tell them I'm in here."

"I won't, Sarah. I swear."

"And don't give them access. Tell them it's been locked all night and will remain locked until they've cleared the place."

"No one goes in there."

"I'll leave when it's clear."

"Stay as long as you need, Sarah." Janet backhanded her tears. "I'm scared. So please stay. I prefer you here."

"You didn't see me. Remember that."

"I didn't see you."

Sarah let the café door close. The lock engaged.

She ran to the kitchen and hunted for tablecloths. After

finding at least six of them, she located a back corner of the café, one of the darkest areas, and piled the tablecloths in a makeshift sleeping bag.

"Good idea."

Sarah jumped at the voice, her hands coming up in a defensive posture.

Lacee Faust was still in her café.

"What the fuck, man? Why are you still here?"

"Couldn't leave."

"Why? I warned you. People died tonight."

"There's a back door to this place. If they shot their way in, I could've left. But I thought I'd stay."

"Still doesn't make sense. Why not leave when you heard gunfire?"

"Sarah, I had a chance to meet you. I figured you'd fix this," she waved her hand back toward the motel, "and there might be a chance we could talk."

"About?" Sarah dropped to the pile of tablecloths and stretched out. She was exhausted, fatigue setting in, the adrenaline leaving her muscles shaky.

"Anything really. Like how you became who you are. How does one *become* a vigilante, anyway?"

"One doesn't."

Lacee frowned. "I was once in an abusive relationship. I found the strength to leave. The woman you are ... no one would dream of trying to push you around."

"Oh, they do. Trust me. I'm pushed around a lot. The difference is I push back."

"I learned that."

"Case by case. Every situation is different. Some people

just need a warning, verbal or physical. Some need a broken nose. Some need a hospital, and some need a coffin." She shrugged. "I never know what's needed until I'm in it, engaged."

"Geez, never looked at it like that."

"This guy you were with, the abusive one, you need this guy taken out? That why you wanted to talk to me?" Sarah crossed her arms and lay back as she listened to the commotion the authorities were making outside the café. "If so, I don't do that sort of thing."

"Nothing like that." Lacee got up and walked toward the restaurant section. "I'll be right back."

"Stay clear of the windows, please."

"I will."

Sarah closed her eyes and focused on her breathing. She considered leaving through that back door Lacee mentioned but figured the cops would be watching it. A moment later, Lacee returned with a bottle of wine and two glasses.

"Smart girl," Sarah said, sitting up. "I'm shaking. I could use a glass of that."

"You? Shaking?"

"Adrenaline always leaves its mark."

Lacee twisted off the cap and poured Sarah a glass, then herself. Once seated back on the tablecloths, Sarah took a couple of sips to cleanse her palate.

More emergency vehicles arrived outside. She listened for indications they would enter the café but heard none.

Lacee sat a few feet from her. "Tell me about you, Sarah."

"Too much to tell. Read about me in the papers."

"I have." Lacee sipped her wine. "When I was young, I thought I'd seen my grandfather."

"He'd passed?"

Lacee nodded. "After he'd passed away, he came to my bedroom, which I shared with my sister." She looked at Sarah and met her gaze. "When I read about you years ago, they said you can hear your dead sister. Vivian? Right?"

Sarah nodded, drank more, then leaned her head back. "Sometimes it's a blessing. Saved my life on many occasions. And sometimes, it's a curse. My sister can piss me off, too."

"I believe in the other side. They're out there, watching over us."

Sarah nodded. "Tell me about your abusive relationship."

Lacee talked for another half an hour about how her boyfriend controlled her, emotionally abused her, and called her names when she walked out—like *she* was the bad one. She had nothing at that moment and was in the process of rebuilding. Her son was doing better, and she had begun to see life as something you had to own, something you had to take charge of to make it what you wanted.

"There's no other way," Sarah said. "Wherever you are in life, you set it up that way, based on your decisions, your acceptance of your surroundings. That extends to the people you allow in your life. You're exactly where you want to be because you put yourself there. If someone else exerts control over you, it's because you've allowed them to. You teach people how to treat you. If you don't like how someone treats you, fix it or get out of their life."

"And that's exactly what I did. No regrets, just lost time.

But I'm making up for that."

Sarah drank the last of her wine, set the glass down, and lay back on the tablecloths. "I might check out soon."

"Ha, funny. Check out. You know, because you're in a motel—"

Someone tried the door.

Sarah bolted upright. The wine rushed to her head, making her dizzy. As tasty and relaxing as it was, maybe she should've waited to drink.

Whoever it was must have left. The door didn't open.

"Don't worry," Lacee said. "We've had cops here before. When the café is closed, they never come in. They've got enough to deal with in the motel itself. They won't be coming in here. Besides, cops only do as much as they *have* to, nothing more."

Sarah nodded. "And if they ask you to leave."

"I'll leave and lock it behind me. You'll be free to sleep until it opens at seven for breakfast."

"Then I better get to sleep."

"Sarah?"

"Yeah?" She eased back onto the floor.

"I'm so glad we met. Thank you for listening to my story. I feel lighter for it."

"We girls have to stick together. I'm the one who is honored, Lacee. It takes guts to do what you did. Well done, woman. And do me a favor." Sarah closed her eyes.

"Anything."

"Find a man. Love again. Live life again. But never, ever let a man, or *anyone* for that matter, walk on you or over you. Ever. Can you do that?"

"Of course."

"I'll tell Vivian to watch over you and come and tell me if you're fucking up," she said, her voice taking on a light tone. "And if you do, I'll come back. To find you. To smack you."

Lacee laughed. "Careful, Sarah. I might just let someone control me to see you again."

"Better not …" Her voice was far off, distant.

"Kidding."

Lacee sounded like she was down a long hallway.

"Sleep, Sarah. I got you."

"Thanks, Lacee. I'm out."

And Sarah drifted off the cliff into sleep.

Chapter 22

Blacken found his wife awake but still groggy from the hit. The goon was still out, his wheezing breath even more labored.

He unhooked her from the wrist restraints and helped her to her feet.

A single siren, muffled somewhat from the basement, stopped in front of the house.

He slipped an arm under Kym's and led her to the back door. When he opened it, the sound of more emergency vehicles drew close.

Without wasting time, he started her toward the back fence. They were lost to the darkness as they moved away from the house, with little light coming from a couple of the windows. They'd get out of this if he could just make the fence.

Kym pulled back several feet from the fence, almost getting away from him.

"Let me go," she said, her voice too loud.

He jerked her toward him until they were nose to nose. "I can't. You're coming with me."

"No. I'm. Not." She struggled to pull away, grunting in a whiny tone.

"Stop fighting me, you bitch." He grabbed her wrists and clamped down. She cried out in pain as he twisted her arms, one over the other. He locked her elbows together, then pulled her to him.

"I'm saving your life, Kym."

She glared at him, the bruise on her face already a large purple abrasion. It would turn yellow in the coming days, an ugly, jaundiced color, and eventually fade—if she lived that long.

"Oh yeah?" she yelled. "How is this saving my life?" She pulled hard to break free, but he held her tight. "You lied to me." Her voice became a cry, a plea. "I loved you. I let you go." She sobbed.

He released his left hand, leaving his stronger one holding her, and retrieved Jensen's note.

"Here. Read this."

He was able to snap it open and hold it up for her in what little light they had.

Cars stopped out front. Sirens turned off. They would be around the house soon, searching the backyard. Officers had probably already breached the front door. Once the dead goon on the top floor was located, a search that included dogs would develop into a manhunt. They needed to leave and get to their cabin to survive this. He could regroup, think about things, and make a new plan later. But first, the cabin.

"That bastard," Kym said. "He set me up."

Blacken nodded. "He waited for you to hear he would kill me and knew you'd break me free. He's gone. Long gone. Those goons were there to silence us. I took care of them."

She stared at him a moment. "Took care of them? As in, you know?"

"No, no, nothing like that. They're knocked out. Unable to hurt us. But we have to leave. Those cops out front are Jensen's men." He started her toward the fence again, slipping the note back into his pocket. Jensen was so sure his plan would work that he didn't think about leaving incriminating evidence behind on the fridge door. Although, he didn't sign the note and could've written it while wearing gloves. If something like this ever made it to court, Blacken was sure Jensen's lawyers could classify the note as inadmissible.

But it would never get to court, and Jensen knew that as much as Blacken did. Jensen had drawn a line in the sand, and whoever crossed it would be killed.

"Where will we go?" Kym asked.

"How about we get in the car and decide? But I can tell you, staying here isn't an option."

The back gate rattled behind them. Lights turned on in several windows. Someone shouted from inside Jensen's huge house.

"Can you climb this fence?" Blacken whispered.

"I don't think so."

"I'll help." He locked his fingers together and bent at the waist, making a step for her foot. "Place your foot here, and I'll boost you up."

The side gate at the house creaked open. Officers ran into the backyard, looking left and right.

"Hurry," he whispered.

She stepped into his hands.

"Now, push up and grab the top of the fence."

"Then what?"

"Hold on until I'm over. Then I'll help you down the other side."

She did as she was told. He lifted her up until she was balancing perilously on the top, her stomach taking all the weight.

He clambered up as the patio door by the kitchen opened, and the backlights of the house turned on, flooding the yard.

He dropped to the other side and grabbed her waist.

"I think someone's at the fence," a man yelled.

With guns raised and flashlights aimed forward, several officers started toward the back of the yard.

Blacken eased her higher, then dragged her over the top of the fence, over his head, until her feet cleared, and she fell into him, almost toppling them both.

"Freeze!" someone yelled.

Kymberly hadn't spoken a word or even grunted. The fence was so far from the house that they couldn't be seen unless they had a flashlight trained on them. The officer probably yelled at the sound and didn't know what he might be walking into.

Been there, done that. A thousand times.

Blacken guided his wife to the large tree a short distance from the fence, slipped behind it, and placed Kym in front of him.

Now, they were invisible to anyone in Jensen's yard. The only way to discover them was to hop the fence, and he was betting on none of the officers doing that in the dark—not without dogs.

Flashlights played across the foliage around them. To Kym's credit, she leaned into Blacken's chest and stayed quiet, controlling her breathing through her open mouth.

They waited like a married couple running from a bar after stiffing them for the bill. They were in this together, the stakes high, evenly distributed now. Kym felt betrayed by Jensen. Kym betrayed Blacken. Ultimately, everyone betrayed everyone, and life went on because that's what people do. They fucked with each other.

As soon as he got Kym to the car, he would betray her trust again. Kym was nothing but a pawn in Blacken and Jensen's game. Jensen played an entirely different game than Blacken, but nevertheless, they were playing with each other, toying with their lives and careers.

And Jensen would lose.

The lights lifted off the bushes and the grass. He waited several more moments, holding Kym close, listening.

The officers by the fence whispered. He couldn't make out anything they were saying. One thing was for sure, though; none of the men climbed the fence.

Maybe they were waiting for dogs. If so, Blacken and his wife would have to make a run for it. But that wouldn't work.

How could they run blindly through the darkened woods? They'd run into trees, trip over branches, and get nowhere fast.

He knew the way back to the car, but they couldn't manage it running. If dogs came, he'd have no choice but to shoot them. And then what?

There was no good ending here. Nothing would work unless the officers moved away from the fence. Far enough away that Blacken and his wife could walk to the path in the moonlight and make it to his car.

Someone yelled something. One of the cops by the fence shouted back for them to repeat themselves.

"We have a body upstairs. Crime lab on the way. Everyone off the scene. They want it secure for analysis. And we'll need everyone's name for the murder log."

"Shit," one of the cops close to the fence muttered.

After a few moments, Blacken eased around the side of the tree.

The back fence was clear. He slipped his hand into hers and guided her to the path. She stumbled a couple of times but held on.

"This doesn't mean anything for us, you know," she said. "Hitting me was a deal breaker."

"I understand. I'll take you to your sister's place. Or anywhere else you want to go."

"Good. As long as we're clear."

"Just don't go back to Jensen."

"I don't plan on it."

"He was using you."

"I know that now."

They made it to his car without trouble. It had to be one or two in the morning. The residential street a few over from Jensen's was quiet and dark, save for a random streetlight.

He stopped by the passenger door and looked up at her, the moon shining on her cheeks, one swollen, one not.

"I'm sorry I hit you."

"No, you're not." She reared back a bit, staring into his eyes.

"For the record. I just wanted to say that."

"Then why did you?"

"I knew what Jensen was up to."

"Bullshit." She tried the door. "Let me in the car, or I'll start walking and find a cab."

He pulled out his keys, placing the kubaton in his grip, the keys protruding at the end.

"I just wanted to apologize for hitting you because—"

He lurched forward, the kubaton coming up, the end of it sticking out half an inch, and jammed it into her temple so hard her head snapped sideways and bounced off the side of the roof's edge.

She stumbled, trying to stay on her feet, her eyes searching for him. He guided her a couple of steps toward the back of the car, pushed the trunk button on the key fob, and then gripped her by the hair.

"Sorry about this, too."

He pulled upward, her head jerking back, then shoved downward as he brought his knee up and connected with her face.

The force of the blow knocked her out for the second time that night. Blacken's wife dropped to his feet.

Once he picked her up and secured her in the trunk of his car, he duct-taped her mouth, wrists, and ankles—a roll of silver duct tape was always in his trunk—and closed the lid.

One last look around, and then he was behind the wheel and driving toward the highway. He was back in business. The plan could go ahead. The only difference now was Jensen had to be dealt with—in the worst possible way.

As he hit the highway and headed north toward cottage country, he realized he had been a Nazi doctor in his past life with the thoughts of the terrible things he was going to do to Jensen.

He turned on the stereo and listened to his Metallica CD. His favorite song was playing: "Blackened."

Like his name. Like his soul.

Chapter 23

Parkman couldn't sleep. Aaron had trouble sleeping but had managed to drift off half an hour ago. Parkman dressed in the hotel bathroom and exited the room without a sound, not wanting to disturb Aaron.

Down in the lobby, he dialed Casper.

"Parkman," Casper answered immediately, resonating charm. "You good?"

"Yeah, fine."

"Something I can do for you?"

"Does the word Blacken mean anything to you?"

"One second," Casper said. Parkman listened to Casper shuffling and moving about. "There. Now, why do you ask? Fill me in."

"You at home?"

"Home office. Just got behind my desk."

Parkman headed toward the corridor that led to the conference rooms, which were empty at this late hour. "I hope I didn't wake you."

"Nonsense. I was up reading. What's this about Blacken?"

"It's a long story, but I'll make it quick." Parkman told him about the strange encounter at the airport with the man in the pickup truck and his warning for Sarah. He brought Casper up to speed on everything Sarah was doing and how she wasn't involved with the prison bus thing, only leaving out the part Sarah made them swear they'd tell no one. For some reason, Vivian had explained that Sarah's final plan and their part in it would not work if anyone outside their circle of three knew about it.

Casper could be trusted not to betray them, but Sarah was adamant, and that was good enough for Parkman.

"Detective Joel Blacken. He's a solid detective."

Parkman stopped walking. "What?"

"And he's suspect numero uno in a murder case that just happened this evening."

"You're kidding."

"You're saying this guy at the airport was running scared, wearing Kevlar? He mentioned Blacken and told you to warn Sarah?"

Parkman plopped down in a chair by the conference room doors of his hotel. "Yeah."

"Parkman, you okay?"

"Yeah."

"Doesn't sound like it."

"Just. Shocked." He swallowed, then licked his dry lips. He missed his toothpicks. Perhaps the front desk could rustle some up for him. "Why would this detective have a thing for Sarah? And murder? Really? Casper, what the hell's going on?"

Casper told Parkman what he knew about Sergeant Travis Jensen and how two men known to police were found in Jensen's house, one dead and one in the hospital with a broken face.

"And this was Blacken?" Parkman asked.

"According to Jensen."

"*According* to Jensen? Meaning there's suspicion he could be lying?"

"Not lying, just not telling the whole truth. He's got video surveillance on his house."

"Oh, man." Parkman placed a hand on his forehead. "You know, Sarah didn't ask for any of this. These people, they keep pulling her back in."

"I know, Parkman. Where is she now?"

"I have no idea."

"You going to see her soon? Get a message to her?"

"Sure. I could try and call her. But she'd take your call as well as mine."

"Last I heard," Casper said, "she was seen at a motel in Mississauga. There was a shootout. People are dead. Four or five. The numbers are still coming in."

Parkman shot up in his chair. "This is out of control."

"At least two, possibly three of the dead are the shooters. Known gang members. According to witnesses, Sarah showed up and tried to get everyone out of the motel, but she was too late. She fought back and killed some of theirs but wasn't fast enough. We lost a couple of civilians, too."

"The media will love this. They won't see Sarah in a good light because of the manhunt, even though witnesses will say different."

"I know. But Parkman, we can't find Sarah. I've tried her number. Nothing. If you see her or hear from her, call me. I can bring her in and keep her safe."

"Keep her safe, Casper? This is Sarah we're talking about." Parkman got to his feet and started for the front desk. He needed a toothpick for sure now. "She's done nothing wrong."

"Every cop in this country is looking for her. After that prison bus thing and now the motel, she'll be the most hunted woman in history."

A lot of what Sarah wanted Parkman and Aaron to do for her was starting to fall together to make perfect sense. The scuba diving training, the boat rental, the address, the lake. Everything Sarah told them to do per her sister. Even the no-weapons rule. Vivian had a plan, and Sarah was her pawn as much as Parkman and Aaron. It was risky, perhaps too risky.

"Parkman?"

"Yeah, sorry. Just thinking. One second."

He reached the front desk and slapped the small silver bell. A door opened behind the counter, and a man slipped out. Parkman lowered the cell phone to his side.

"Are there any toothpicks around?"

"Toothpicks? I'm sure the restaurant has some, but they're closed until breakfast. I'm sorry, sir."

"Shit." He turned away and brought the phone to his ear.

"Casper, I'll get ahold of Sarah. Tell her to reach out to you. Maybe there's a way out of this." Or maybe they do it Vivian's way.

"She's in over her head. A lot of dead bodies in a short span of time, Parkman. I know she has nothing to do with it, but the boys above me will want answers, and as of right now, I have none."

When Parkman turned back around, the front desk clerk had disappeared.

"I understand. Thanks, Casper. We'll work this out."

Parkman ended the call. The restaurant door was open. The clerk said it wouldn't be open until breakfast.

Then, the clerk emerged.

"Toothpicks," he said, holding up a small container.

"Oh, you're an angel."

Parkman grabbed a handful, stuck one in each corner of his mouth, stuffed the rest in his back pocket, slapped the clerk on the shoulder in thanks, and started for the stairs.

He would get some sleep and start shopping in the morning. They would buy everything Sarah instructed and head north to rent that boat.

The only way to save Sarah Roberts was to do it her way. He'd known her long enough to know that if he tried to change her mind or the plan, things would go wrong, and Sarah would pay for it if things went wrong.

But forget all that, he told himself. What Sarah explained made more sense now than when they first heard it.

He bounded up the stairs toward his hotel room, knowing he would be instrumental in Sarah's death.

At least, that's what everyone would think, and he was

fine with it.

He rolled the toothpicks in his mouth to change sides and felt much better about everything.

Chapter 24

BLACKEN MADE IT TO his summer cabin before sunrise. Kym barely made a sound in the trunk after waking, which probably meant she knew he would let her out when he was good and ready. She'd grunted a couple of times and kicked the underside of the trunk, but he'd only turned up his music.

No one would come to the cottage. No one knew he and Kym owned it. Well, maybe a couple of officers who had come up for a weekend once, but it wasn't on the books, and even then, Blacken had told them it wasn't his.

The remote cabin was secluded, surrounded by the thick trees of northern Ontario, in the heart of cottage country. Neighbors' cottages were half a kilometer away at least, and they only came up on weekends.

No one would bother them. No one would wander by. No

one would hear a thing if noise became an issue.

Blacken grabbed his cell phone and the burner. Outside the car, he took a deep breath of early morning pine, held it, and then let it out, relaxing in the moment. It had been a tough few days. The set up to the prison bus attack, the question of whether or not Russell would do the job. Then Kym called off their marriage and his frantic search for her. Imagine Jensen holding him captive in his basement. Was that just to see if Kym would bring the key? Or was Jensen genuinely intent on killing him?

The cool morning breeze reminded him that his pants were still damp. It had only been five hours since he'd wet himself.

Once Kym was secure, he'd shower, change, and then nap for a bit.

He popped the trunk. She glared at him, eyes filled with anger and hatred.

"You don't know my limits," he said. "You wanted to test me." He pulled out his kubaton and slid out a small knife from inside it. "Blacken always wins. And when I say that name, just for clarity, I mean me. You're not a Blacken anymore." He leaned in toward her ankles and placed the knife on the duct tape. "You gave up that right when you fucked my boss." He yanked, the tiny knife easily slicing through the tape. "And if you're not a Blacken, then you're not family. And if you're not family, and you're hurting me, then you're my enemy." He slit her wrists free.

She tried to smack him, but he easily dodged it. After grasping at the tape on her mouth, she yanked it off with one fast pull.

"How dare you, Joel?" she blurted. "I let you go. I released you from Jensen's basement."

He stood over her, looking into the trunk of his car, shaking his head. "I shouldn't have been tied up in the first place. I was only there because of you."

She grabbed the edge of the trunk, twisted until she was on her knees, and then climbed out, mumbling something about being cramped up in the trunk. She moaned as she hit the ground and stood to her full height slowly, hands on her lower back.

"You'll pay for this, Joel."

"I already have." He grabbed her wrist. "Come with me."

She recoiled but didn't fight too hard. She knew he had the upper hand. She also had to know where they were, and that screaming wouldn't bring anyone anytime soon.

He clamped hard on her wrist all the way to the front door, unlocked it with one hand, and shoved the door open. He guided her inside, flicked on the lights, then slammed the door shut behind them.

Her eyes flickered toward the back door, then to the living room. He saw it, though. The smallest tinge of hope she might outrun him.

"How about we take a moment," he said. "Regroup, decide what to do."

She looked at him, a smirk on her lips. She was in placate mode. He knew her very well.

"That sounds good. Would you like me to put on coffee or tea?"

He laughed. It came softly at first, but then he couldn't control it. A full-on belly laugh, eyes watering. He leaned into the wall. After a few moments, he collected himself, wiping his eyes.

"Domestic bliss, eh?" He laughed again but tried to suppress it. "Fuck you, Kym. In fact, this sounds better. Fuck you, *ex*-wife."

He shoved her. She stumbled back, lost her balance, and fell to the floor, hitting her shoulder blade on the side of the wooden coffee table. Her face scrunched up in pain. A small gasp, then a deep moan, escaped her lips.

He approached her.

"Don't touch me," she shouted, pain lacing her strained voice.

He took a chunk of her hair and pulled her toward the basement stairs. She squealed and crawled on the floor, trying to lessen the pressure on her scalp.

The basement access was a rectangular wooden door in the floor—like a trap door—covered with a small carpet. He kicked the carpet aside and swung open the door, then pulled her toward the top of the wooden stairs, releasing her so she didn't fall headfirst to the bottom.

"What are you doing?" she screamed at him.

Without responding, he grabbed her arm and started down the stairs. She was able to clamber to her knees on the floor, then to her feet by the second stair, and followed him down quickly. Her balance maintained, she made it to the bottom unscathed.

The add-on basement was something of an afterthought for Blacken. He had some guys dig it out many years ago to be used as a small wine cellar. It was by no means the kind of basement that could be found in finished homes in any urban setting, more like the earthy, dirt-walled cellars of Europe where fine wines were stored. He never got to the wine stage, leaving it as a dirt-floored hole under the cabin.

There were no windows, doors, or way out except the flat door in the floor near the back of their living room they had just used. The door locked from above. The thick seventies shag rug muffled any sound from below.

"You can't leave me down here," she pleaded.

He started for the stairs. "You won't die, and I'll bring you food and water."

"I'm supposed to trust you?" Her voice rose an octave.

"Doesn't matter."

He was on the second stair when she ran into him. He never heard her coming across the dirt floor.

Blacken smacked into the steps as his ex-wife grabbed at his shirt, his hair, his face.

He swung around, protecting his face. He pushed her away with his foot, knocking her off balance as she stumbled to her rump.

A part of him wanted to get out of his pissed-in clothes, have some food, and go to bed. Another part wanted to walk over and beat the shit out of her.

He chose food and a bed.

By the time he got to the top of the stairs—unaccosted this time—Kym was crying like a baby. He could only imagine the life she used to have compared to her previous twelve hours. How could she ever imagine being knocked out, bound and gagged, and a virtual prisoner in her own cellar?

Blacken locked the door and pulled the carpet over it,

suppressing the sound of her sobs. He'd done it. He got to her. She was his until the end game.

Now for stage two. It was time to contact Sarah Roberts.

He removed his filthy jeans and shirt and picked up the burner phone.

He dialed Sarah's number from memory, having gotten it under false pretenses from a fellow officer and committing it to memory.

The phone rang six times before going to voicemail.

"Shit."

This only worked if she answered. He opened a bottle of tequila, poured a shot, drank it back, poured another, and moved to the sofa.

He could finally relax. No one knew where he was. His hideout from society. No matter what story Jensen spun, no cops came to this hidden cabin in the woods.

He dialed Sarah's number again and put it on speakerphone.

On the fifth ring, something clicked.

He leaned forward on the couch, staring at the phone, waiting, listening.

Finally, he said, "Hello?"

"I've been waiting for your call, Blacken," Sarah said. "I'm coming for you."

Chapter 25

The phone startled her awake. Then it stopped ringing. Moments later, it rang again.

Sarah waited a couple of rings before she answered it, opening her eyes in the motel café.

Vivian whispered what to say.

"I've been waiting for your call, Blacken. I'm coming for you."

The line died.

She set her phone down and flicked it to vibrate. Vivian had explained what she was to do. It wasn't just a gang attack at a motel. There was much more to do. It would be a busy day on the run, then heading north. She only hoped Parkman and Aaron were doing well with their tasks. Everything depended on them being at the right place at the right time.

She rolled to her side and sat up.

"Coffee?"

Sarah looked up at her host. "Lacee. You stayed?"

"All night." She grinned at Sarah. "Couldn't have someone coming in here looking for you when you were alone sleeping." She poured a cup. "I slept a bit in front of the door."

"You didn't have to."

"There's a lot of things I don't have to do, Sarah, believe me." She handed Sarah the coffee. "Cream and sugar?"

"Black." Sarah took a sip. It tasted great. "What time is it? What time do you open?"

"We open in twenty minutes."

"There a place I can wash up?" Sarah asked.

"The woman at the front desk last night left me this."

Lacee handed Sarah a room key.

"Janet gave you a room key for me?"

Lacee nodded. "She also told me to tell you that she was sorry for not trusting you and that it's something she'll have to live with."

"That's got to be hard." Sarah frowned. "Hey, wait. If you had a room key, why wasn't I in a soft bed all night? Why am I sleeping on the floor?"

"Because in here, I could watch over you, and no one was investigating the café." She waved at the motel. "Every room was scoured by cops last night. They would have found you."

Sarah sipped more coffee, then nodded. "Makes sense."

"When you're done with your coffee, head to room 101. There's a shower, or bath, whatever you prefer, and there'll be a change of clothes."

Surprised, she glanced up at Lacee again. "Clothes?"

"You should change to stay under the radar."

"I don't have an issue with that, but where did you get clothes that'll fit me in the middle of the night?"

"I didn't. Yet."

"Huh?"

"My mother works at a clothing store in the mall. She went in this morning and snatched several sizes of pants, shirts, and other things for you to pick from. She'll be here in," Lacee checked her watch, "about fifteen minutes." She looked back at Sarah. "Mom's coming for breakfast. You're having a shower, changing, and having breakfast with us."

Sarah hadn't felt this welcomed from a complete stranger in a long time.

"I'm usually not at a loss for words, but thank you, Lacee."

"Janet and I thank you, Sarah. We felt we had to do something." Lacee grabbed the coffee pot and refilled Sarah's cup. "Everyone has it wrong about you."

"Tell me about it."

They exchanged a friendly, knowing glance, and then Lacee turned toward the front. "Look, I have to open the doors soon. It'd be better if you're in room 101 before that in case customers are standing and waiting at the door, which is usually the case."

Sarah stretched, pocketed her phone, and got to her feet. "I understand."

"When my mom gets here, I'll bring the clothes to your room."

Lacee walked her to the door, told her which corridor to take, then unlocked the door.

Sarah crossed the motel lobby, keeping her face turned away from the morning clerk. Once in her room, she showered and stayed wrapped in a towel while watching the morning news for twenty minutes until there was a soft rapping on the door.

She muted the TV and checked the peephole. She let Lacee in and examined the cache of clothes.

"I can't thank you and your mom enough, Lacee. This is perfect."

Lacee plopped down on the side of the bed. "Where are you headed next?"

She looked up briefly, then back down at the shirts sprawled out on the bed.

"Can't say, really. Wherever my sister takes me."

"Must be cool, hearing from the other side."

Sarah shook her head. "Not really. Sometimes I hate what I do."

"If you could go back, you know, change your life, do something else, be someone else, would you?"

Sarah stopped what she was doing and tightened the towel around her. "I've never been asked that."

"Well?"

She glanced over at the silent TV. An image of the front of a house in Barrie where a dead body was found the previous evening was splashed across the screen. As the reporter talked, the words scrolled along the bottom. The police were looking for a person of interest, but they weren't offering names yet.

She glanced back at Lacee, who hadn't taken her eyes off Sarah.

"I wouldn't change a thing," Sarah said. "I'd do it again and will continue doing it as long as I'm able. But," she raised her voice on that last word along with her finger, "I would like a vacation first. A month, maybe two, to do nothing but drink and sleep. Oh, and spend time with Aaron."

"Your boyfriend." It was a statement more than a question.

"You know a lot about me."

"The news. They tell all."

"Imagine so."

She picked an average pair of blue jeans and a black shirt. Of the clothes Lacee's mom had brought, they would work the best.

After changing into them, she turned to Lacee. "What's your mom's name?"

"Karen."

"Tell Karen I said thanks."

"You can tell her yourself. We have breakfast ready. Come to the café. We'll eat in the back, in the employee lunch room."

"You sure?"

"Sarah, you have to eat."

"Then I have to leave. I need to be downtown by noon."

"Plenty of time."

Sarah met Karen, had breakfast, and they chatted up a storm. By eleven, Karen offered to drive Sarah downtown.

She said her goodbyes, promised to return, hugged Lacee and thanked her for everything, then got in the car and was dropped off near Yonge and Shuter Streets, near the large mall where the Rapturites attacked her and Rod Howley all those years ago.

At noon, she was exactly where she was supposed to be. She'd bought a ball cap and set the bill low, covering most of her face.

And she waited. She waited for a girl in a red shirt that said *O'Neill* on it.

The day was young. There was a lot to do, lives to save, and people to hurt.

And, according to Vivian, she needed to be in cottage country on a certain road in the middle of the night.

She still had no idea why but suspected it had something to do with Blacken, who had called her that morning but had not yet called back.

Soon, everything would come together. And Sarah would be free.

The brunette wearing the *O'Neill* shirt was right on time. She stepped out of the shadows of a tattoo shop directly in front of the brunette.

"Your little brother is in a lot of trouble."

The brunette frowned. "What? Who are you?" She tried to walk around Sarah, but Sarah stepped in her path again.

"Rob Russell is your brother, right? You're Jessica."

"Yeah, but who are you?"

"I'm trying to save Rob's life."

"How so? He's a cop. I'm sure he can take care of himself."

"Call him. Warn him. Tell him to stay away from Blacken. That's the message. If he doesn't, he will die."

"Those are strong words." Jessica's voice rose a pitch. "You can't stop people in the middle of the street and say shit like that."

Sarah leaned in close. "Just did. And keep your voice down." She gripped Jessica's shoulders tight and stared into her eyes. "Call him. Or live with his death on your hands."

"Oh yeah? How's he going to die? You tell me that, eh?" She was screaming now. People were looking. Too much attention. "Are you threatening a cop? Maybe we should call the police, let them sort it out."

"Goodbye, Jessica. Call your brother. Save his life." Sarah moved away, then shouted over her shoulder. "If you don't call him, you killed him."

Sarah turned a corner and headed to her next person, her next warning.

It would only get worse as the day wore on.

But she was ready for a day of fighting. A day of setting things right, one person at a time.

Chapter 26

BLACKEN WOKE MID-AFTERNOON and checked his burner phone. He hadn't blocked the number because the burner would be crushed and thrown away within a day or two, but Sarah hadn't tried to call him back. On his regular phone, several colleagues had left messages pleading with him to call in and let them hear his side. The investigator in charge at Jensen's house had left messages as well, explaining that no response from Blacken would not look good.

He deleted all the messages, made coffee, and went out to sit on the front veranda to enjoy the summer morning air.

Things had taken a terrible turn, but he'd been able to steer everything back on course. His ex-wife—he wouldn't use her first name again—was where she was supposed to be. He was where he'd planned to be, and soon, he hoped Sarah would be where she planned to be.

Yet there was something about Russell that still worried Blacken. He'd pulled the trigger on the prison bus and spun that tale very well. But would he nab Parkman, take him off the street like he was supposed to? Would he pick him up at the airport and deposit him in a holding cell for processing on a bogus charge so Blacken could have something to negotiate with Sarah?

If not, if Parkman was a free man, what would he have to convince Sarah to come to have a sit-down?

His call that morning was a precursor. I can get to your people. I have the authority. Don't test me. And after Parkman was off the street, he could have his old partner grab Aaron for questioning. Then, another call to Sarah to meet.

But that didn't happen. And wouldn't now.

When he'd called her, she had surprised him. Not only did she know who was calling, but she was waiting for his call. She knew about him. Possibly even where his cabin was. And she was coming for him.

Impossible.

But didn't people say she had psychic powers?

Psychic powers? He laughed to himself and sipped more of his coffee.

Why was she always in the thick of things if she had psychic powers? Why not *know* the future and avoid the shit?

"Yeah, right. Psychic powers, my ass."

He'd seen her picture. She was quite hot. If he had the chance and she was in his cabin, maybe he'd teach her what a real man could do for a woman. He was *legally separated*, after all.

He thought about making breakfast and taking some down to the ex-wife but then thought better of it. He'd just make breakfast, and that would be that. It wouldn't kill her to not eat for the morning. Maybe she'd even lose a few pounds if he put her on the starvation diet.

After breakfast, he'd work on the large, old hole in the backyard. He needed it ready in case someone advanced on his cabin from that direction.

He sipped his coffee and grinned to himself, feeling euphoric, triumphant. He'd done it. Hidden himself in a place no one knew and had his ex-wife in her little prison cell.

He rose from the deck chair, stretched, and wandered off the side of the deck to the back of the cabin to survey the hole. It was still there, the sides fallen down in places. He would shore up certain areas and cover them with the camouflage tarp, which clicked into place at the four corners. It would hold leaves and twigs on top, but not a person.

Step on it and drop six feet in a second.

Another laugh escaped him, a deep guttural laugh.

He pivoted and laughed again. He couldn't contain himself. The maniacal laughter spewed out, and he dumped the rest of his coffee onto the grass.

After several moments to collect himself, Blacken returned to the cabin to make a hearty breakfast for a hard day's work.

He had to prepare for Sarah's arrival, whether that night, the next, or the one after.

She would come, of that he was sure.

Or he'd call in a favor to the Santa Rosa Police

Department in California and have Sarah's parents picked up for questioning.

"I mean," he said to himself, "their daughter is the source of a massive manhunt in Canada. Maybe they could shed some light on where she might be."

When he entered the cabin, Blacken was still laughing, his eyes wet with tears.

Chapter 27

Within fifteen minutes, Sarah had located her next target, which seemed to be getting easier. Vivian was in her head again, acting like a human GPS. She whispered which way to walk and how fast. On autopilot, robot-like, Sarah strode to her target as if she possessed psychic magnetism, drawn by a force, not of this world, not of this plane.

In front of a liquor store, she stopped beside a man smoking against a wall.

"Got a smoke?" she asked.

"Fuck off," he said.

She stepped in closer, out of the blazing sun, so she didn't have to squint when talking to him.

"Now that's not very polite."

"What part of fuck and off don't you get?" the man said,

pushing off the wall, his chest thrust out.

That posturing look, the peacock, the feathers, almost made her laugh. She knew this guy shied away from fights. He only acted tough. One bop on the nose, and he'd drop to the ground like a sniveling baby.

Tomorrow, he planned to rob the liquor store. Him and his heroin-addict friend. The heroin friend would get jumpy and stab one of the clerks. It would be a deep wound, severing an artery. People would die. And all because they wanted one more fix.

They would be caught later that night. Jail would be bad for them. Both men would die in prison. On the other hand, if he walked away, he would eventually kick the drug habit and lead a somewhat productive life.

As far as Vivian could see, that was how it was to play out.

"How about this?" Sarah said, leaning inches from his thrust-out chest. "You give me a smoke, and I won't tell anyone what you're planning."

"What?" he stammered, then looked left and right as if cops were inbound. He met her gaze. "You don't know shit, bitch."

She held up her left hand, face height, for him to look at. Dutifully, he did.

Then she bitch-slapped him with her right hand so hard his head bumped into the wall behind him.

His knees bent slightly as his hand raced to his face. He moaned, and his eyes met hers.

"What was that for?" he asked.

"Don't call me a bitch. Next time, I'll throat punch you."

She leaned closer still. "After that, I go for the balls. Then I cut you."

"What the fuck, lady? Back off."

He tried to shove her away, but she dodged his hand easily.

"Tomorrow," she whispered, "when you walk in there," she nodded toward the liquor store, "I'll be waiting to kill you and your friend, Ernesto. You want that, Winters?"

His eyes widened, and he straightened up. "You know Ernesto? How do you know my name—what the fuck, man? Hey, how do you know my name?"

"Leave town, asshole. Rob that store tomorrow, and you and Ernesto won't make it out alive."

"What are you, liquor store security or something?"

She eased back into the sunshine. "Something like that."

She waited for Vivian's confirmation. After a moment, she got it. He wouldn't rob the store. In fact, he didn't trust Ernesto anymore and wouldn't take his calls later that night. It was over. The man would move on with his life.

Sarah smiled at him. "See you on Richmond Street."

As she walked away, he said after her, "What the hell does that mean?"

Without answering, she trudged up the sidewalk with only ten minutes to go before she met with a man named Percy, whose life would be ruined later that night because of an affair.

"This is exhausting work, Vivian," Sarah said out loud. "I won't be able to keep up this pace for long. And why am I telling everyone about Richmond Street?"

Vivian just explained that if she could have her save a

hundred people, one at a time per day, it wouldn't be enough. The betrayal would be complete. Sarah's name was tarnished for all to see, her life forfeited.

One by one, in the public's eyes, laying the groundwork, Sarah had to prove them wrong before it was too late.

She trudged north on Yonge Street, weaving between the crowds in search of Percy and telling Vivian she was out of her mind.

"I have nothing to prove and will only do this a few more times today. People have to deal with fate, just like everyone else. And Vivian, maybe you missed the point the other day —I need a break."

And you'll get one, Sarah. A long break ...

Sarah didn't like the sound of that.

Chapter 28

By mid-afternoon, Blacken had finished with the hole. The tarp clamped on easily enough, and he'd camouflaged it expertly. Even in the bright daylight, he couldn't tell there was a four-foot by six-foot hole in the ground, as deep as six to eight feet in most places.

On the back porch, he drank beer and listened to nothing. The silence at the cabin was overwhelming. It was too far from the highway to hear trucks. It was too far from town to hear any hustle, bustle, or cars backfiring. The neighbors were also far away, and the closest cabins on this dead-end road were empty.

He was completely alone with the ex-wife hoarse from screaming in the cellar. While making breakfast, he swore she shouted something but didn't care what. He'd toss her a morsel of food at dinner. Fuck her if she thought she could beat him.

Exhausted, his muscles fatigued from the effort with the hole, he opened another beer and considered taking a nap. He grabbed his burner phone and saw no missed calls. None from Sarah or Rob. Did Russell have Parkman yet?

Wasn't Parkman supposed to have flown out of Toronto already?

He would try Rob's number after his nap.

He checked his personal phone and saw forty-two missed calls. More colleagues, more crime-scene cops. Even one from the ex-wife's friend, wondering where she was. Her sister, Apryl, had called, too.

Hadn't the news raised the alarm about Sarah Roberts yet? The suspicion that she was responsible for the prison bus attack and had a hand in the disappearance of Kymberly Blacken?

He shrugged and finished his beer. He would clarify that when he emerged from the woods in a week and explained everything. How Jensen had been cheating with Blacken's wife. The plot against him. The kidnapping, his escape.

But most of all, Sarah's part in it all.

For it all to come together, all Sarah had to do was visit him at his cabin—and by her own admission, she was on her way.

But first, a nap. He wanted to be well rested in case Sarah came that evening.

A woman like Sarah would arrive under the cover of night.

If he were her, he certainly would.

Blacken entered the cabin, bolted the front door, and headed straight for the bedroom.

When he woke, he would make coffee, then dinner.

And maybe, just maybe, he would give that ex-wife of his something to eat.

Maybe …

Chapter 29

SHE WAITED IN HIDING until Vivian told her to step out. A well-dressed man stopped in his tracks and then tried to skirt around her. He mumbled an apology, kept staring at the ground, and continued walking away from Sarah.

It would be easier to stay quiet and let life work itself out. Vivian prodded, Sarah responded.

"Percy?"

The man's step faltered, and he glanced around. After a moment, he kept walking.

Sarah started after him. "Percy?"

This time, he stopped and turned around. "Do I know you?"

She threw her arms out to the side. "You don't remember me? After all this time?"

Confusion masked his despair. Undoubtedly, he was completely bewildered about who the mid-twenties blonde girl was.

"We were neighbors years ago," Sarah said.

"We were? Where?"

"Back when you lived in Oshawa."

He frowned and stepped aside as camera-wielding tourists walked past him. "I lived there over eight years ago."

Vivian dropped data on people like she was leaking ectoplasm, but only when it furthered Vivian's plan, her cause.

"Then it is you. We lived on Nonquon Road in north Oshawa. You had apartment 802, and I was down the hall in apartment 806. You don't remember me?"

The frown never left his face. "I'm sorry, can't say that I do."

"Didn't you meet your wife there?"

That hit a nerve. The despair on his face was all for Tanya, who seemed distant lately. So distant that he hardly saw her. After a fight over a month ago, she had stopped sleeping in their bed. He hadn't been able to focus on his work and had taken several sick days. While Tanya was out having an affair, Percy was losing his mind with no end in sight. Later that night, Tanya would sleep with a new man she had just met on an internet dating site. That man had herpes, and Tanya would become infected.

If Percy got herpes, his life would fall apart through no fault of his own. If he didn't, and he left Tanya, he would eventually prosper, find love again, and ultimately have kids.

Sarah saw it all and wondered how to convince him to

leave Tanya that day. Then Vivian told her how.

"Listen to me, Percy."

"Okay. I'm listening."

"I'm a private investigator."

"You are?" His eyes widened slightly.

"We need to talk. Hungry?"

"No. I feel sick."

"Percy, you need to eat. Come on." She grabbed his arm and led him to a restaurant a few doors down. "Give me fifteen minutes. I'll buy lunch. Then go back to your despair over Tanya."

He jerked his arm out of her grasp.

"You know my wife?"

Sarah turned back to him. "I know a helluva lot more than that. I know your past and present and what you'll do in the future."

"What is this? Some kind of ghost from Christmas past shit?"

"Something like that." She opened the door to the restaurant. "Free lunch? Fifteen minutes? Then you're on your way, and you'll never see me again."

He waited a couple of heartbeats, staring at her. Vivian whispered that he was sold. Just give him time. Sarah waited, knowing she had time. One more visit later that afternoon, then she had a ride waiting to take her north.

Percy put one foot in front of the other and stopped just inside the door, uncomfortably close to her.

"That part about Oshawa and being neighbors was a lie, right?" he paused, then added, "Truth or I walk."

"The truth is, you lived in Oshawa in apartment 802. The

other part was made up to get your attention."

He continued into the restaurant, saying over his shoulder, "I knew it because I would've remembered you. No way I would forget those intense eyes, that hair."

She followed him inside. "Flirting, Percy?"

He glanced at her. "No. Truth-telling. Can't a guy compliment a woman without it being part of some hashtag movement anymore? Whoever you are, you're an attractive woman. All I'm saying is, I would've remembered that." He looked around. "You've got fifteen minutes. Where are we sitting?"

Sarah pointed at a table, and they headed that way. She liked this guy even more—and her role in helping him, for that matter.

She'd persuade him to ditch his wife and move on, even if she had to beat it into him.

Chapter 30

PARKMAN AND AARON HAD rented another vehicle using Benjamin's credit card, this time without telling him. They joked about how at least Benjamin wasn't being shot at and laughed as they headed north on Highway 400 out of Toronto.

"Feel odd leaving Sarah behind?" Parkman asked. "I mean, you two were supposed to be on vacation by now."

Aaron stared out his window, the hand with the missing finger at his lips, picking at the short facial growth he hadn't trimmed in days.

"It's more than odd." He faced Parkman. "Not only is Sarah doing what Vivian asks, as she always does, but now we are. I know Sarah trusts her sister, but that part is still somewhat hard for me."

"Yeah, to a degree, me too."

Aaron turned back to the window. "Vivian warned Sarah about a huge betrayal of some kind but won't tell her who it is or why they betrayed her. What if it's Vivian this time, and she's sent us out of town where we won't be helpful whatsoever?"

"Not likely, Aaron." Parkman checked his mirrors and changed lanes to get out from behind a slow-moving truck. "Vivian wouldn't do that. If she were, in fact, getting us out of town, it would be to further Sarah's narrative. Meaning, we would've been in the way by staying. I believe in what we're doing. This has to work, and it makes sense."

"How does it make sense?"

"If what Sarah said about the lake is true, then we had better be there, or she'll die. I mean, Aaron, she told us she'd be unconscious when we got to her. That's a lot of detail to fuck around with."

"Don't get me wrong. I'm here, aren't I? It's just that I always feel better on the ground, working alongside Sarah, alongside the authorities, stepping in where I can. Even having my boys with me. This take-off north shit bugs me."

"Understood. I'm in the same boat." He glanced over at Aaron, then in the rearview mirror at the rented boat they pulled behind them on a trailer. "So to speak."

Aaron didn't smile.

They drove in silence for a while until they passed Barrie and Orillia. Just short of Gravenhurst, Parkman pulled into a Tim Hortons on the side of the highway.

"Need a bathroom and a coffee," he said.

Aaron nodded. "Me too."

When the car was parked, Aaron turned to him. "I'm not much of a swimmer. You think this'll work?"

"It has to work. We don't have any other option."

"But if we extricate her before that, as Sarah said, then we don't have to do the water thing?"

"That's right. But don't forget, she felt the only way was the water thing. That's what would seal her fate. Remember what the goal is here."

"Yeah, I remember. How could I forget?" He opened his door to get out.

"Then repeat it to me."

He eased his door back until it was sitting ajar. "We have to let Sarah die, have the funeral, and be done with all of this shit for it to truly go away."

"And as you recall, she made us swear to do what she asked."

Aaron stared at his friend, his brother. "I'm in. All the way. But I didn't agree to like it."

"Neither did I, Aaron, neither did I."

They exited the rental and entered the coffee shop, the weight on their shoulders making them both slump.

Chapter 31

Blacken called Rob Russell on the burner phone after his nap and again after dinner. Each time, he received no answer.

"Dammit." He slammed the burner down on the counter.

If he couldn't get confirmation that Russell had picked up Parkman, what could he tell Sarah to get her to come to the cabin? The *threat* of taking Parkman? He could still call in the favor to pick up Sarah's parents, but according to the news, Detective Joel Blacken and his wife had disappeared. Blacken was wanted for questioning regarding the incident at Jensen's home. How could he call the Santa Rosa police now?

He couldn't call in any other capacity than a professional one. That's just not how it worked.

So, he would wait. No one knew where he was. For now,

he was safe. A place to think and work things out.

He dialed Russell again.

No answer.

He thought about calling Sarah and telling her to come get him, but why would she? Why not just send the authorities and look like the good girl?

No, that wouldn't work.

On the news, Sarah was also wanted in connection with the gang-related shooting at a Mississauga motel. The news had made it clear, due to eyewitness accounts, that Sarah was not a suspect in the case. She was just wanted for questioning to clear up several issues. Sarah's picture was pasted on every news channel, every station. She wouldn't get far. They'd have her within twenty-four hours unless she was good at disguising herself and didn't attempt to take any kind of public transportation, enter a casino where they have facial recognition cameras, or try to cross a border.

Maybe he could offer her refuge. Perhaps that would get her to his cabin.

He decided to break his silence and call Jensen back.

The other end picked up on the fourth ring.

He considered the possibility the call would be recorded.

"Hello," Jensen said. "Anyone there?"

"When I get back, the truth will come out, Jensen."

"Blacken? Where are you?"

"The truth won't set you free, Jensen. You're going to jail."

"Just come in. Tell me where you are, and I'll come get you myself."

"Fuck you. You tried to kill me. Your reign is over."

"That's great, Blacken. Just come in. Tell me where you are."

He ended the call feeling like he was in high school. Why the hell did he call Jensen? To piss him off? To rile him up?

Blacken wanted to lash out at someone. Jensen had derailed his plans, and now he had to fight his way back. Russell probably hadn't done his job, which would eventually get him killed. He owed a lot of money to powerful people. Those tasks relieved him of that debt, providing Russell did as he was told. If he hadn't, Russell's debt still stood, and Blacken had no way to confirm anything.

He would wait until later that night. He could even wait until the morning. Maybe Russell would reach out and get in touch.

If not, Blacken was idling on an island, getting nothing done. He had to be more proactive and more results-oriented.

He set both phones on the counter and poured himself a shot of bourbon. If he was going to hibernate in the cabin another night, he might as well enjoy it.

The ex-wife shouted something from below.

He shot back the bourbon and poured another.

She shouted again.

"Oh yeah, I forgot to feed you," he whispered to himself. "Maybe tomorrow."

He poured more bourbon.

Chapter 32

Sarah exited the restaurant, knowing Percy would go home and start packing his suitcases. The man had wept for his loss, but it was a cleansing cry.

She had a burger and fries and was ready for her last person of the day before she headed north. He was a painter. A man who would do quite well in his time. A man with a lot of childhood pain and a hair-trigger temper. A man who had made a few mistakes recently.

Toronto's streets were busier as the afternoon edged into the evening. Tourists crowded the sidewalks at Yonge and Bloor. Sarah had enough time to stroll along Bloor until she reached Church Street, where she took a right and headed south. After walking for several minutes, she prepared to meet Adam DePont. She had one minute left to get in the zone, breathe in, breathe out, and be ready.

She leaned against a dirty brick wall and watched people walk by, the local stores bustling with traffic. The retailers were crammed together, all the buildings touching each another like a modern Amsterdam. Tiny grocery outlets, small kiosks, vape stores, and convenience stores. Even a small hardware store.

She checked the time. Only seconds left until Adam arrived. She watched the people around her and wondered if anyone would try to be a hero.

She counted the rest of the seconds off in her head until Vivian told her to move.

Sarah pushed off the wall, almost bumped into Adam DePont as he moved in front of her, lowered her center of gravity, and then drove a fist into his gut. He bent at the waist, air racing from his mouth, his eyes registering shock and surprise.

Sarah's elbow shot up and clipped the side of his face. Before he had a chance to respond, she grabbed his left arm, shoved him to the ground, lifted his finger, and, in one swift movement, stepped on it, forcing the finger backward.

There was a sickening crunch.

Adam DePont screamed.

She let him go and stepped back. Everyone nearby stared, giving them room. Adam wailed, his good hand clasped to the wrist of the hand with the broken index finger.

"What'd you do … that for?" he shouted as soon as he could regain his voice.

Sarah moved closer to Adam and shouted back, "That's for what you did to Valorie."

"She put you up to this?"

His broken finger sat at an odd angle.

"I've never met Valorie, but I know what you did to her. The beatings, her broken fingers. How could you, Adam?"

Adam glanced around. No one came to his aid. Someone shouted for her to finish him off. A man stood with his cell phone up, probably recording. Sarah was sure it would hit YouTube later.

"How can I work like this?" Adam held his broken finger up to show her. "I'm a painter. I'm left-handed. This'll set me back months, perhaps longer."

Sarah shrugged. "Touch Valorie again, and I'll set you back for the rest of your life. You can live without hands, right?" She offered him a wry smile, then eased back and melted into the crowd.

What she had done was over the top in most circumstances, but not this time. Adam had lost his temper and beat Valorie—twice. She was a fool for staying with him after the first time, but last week, he had broken her hand. Now they were even.

But that wasn't the entire story.

Vivian explained that Adam's art studio was in an old Richmond Street building near Spadina Avenue. When Adam was scheduled to paint at his art studio in approximately forty hours, there would be a car accident involving a propane truck. Through a freak accident, the propane truck will explode. The only fatality would be inside an art studio on the first floor of the Richmond Street building. Vivian showed Sarah an image of the newspaper the day after the accident, Adam DePont's mug on the cover.

That image had enabled her to identify him instantly.

With a broken finger, he wouldn't be painting at his studio during the accident. That, and the studio's keys she stole from his pocket when he was on the ground.

She wasn't sure why Vivian told her to steal the keys from Adam, but she did as she was told.

She couldn't stop everything from happening; the world was too big. But she could change one life, one perspective at a time.

It would be no great loss if Adam discovered what happened to his art studio. Most of his finished pieces were in his apartment—he only worked there.

A group of people watched her as she headed back toward Yonge Street. She strode along on a side road beside a city parking area.

Someone shouted, "Hey, isn't that Sarah Roberts?"

Unable to help herself, she looked at the person who shouted. A group of rough-looking men nodded at her and started across the street. Others followed.

"Shit." She broke into a run and hit Yonge Street in a full sprint. The second she turned the corner, a door opened as someone exited a building.

Sarah grabbed the door, jumped inside, pulled the door closed, and locked the thumb latch.

"Can we help you?"

She spun around to face a woman holding a pool cue in one hand and a beer in the other. She was in an empty pool hall and bar other than the woman speaking to her and a woman behind the bar.

"Sure. That looks good." She nodded at the woman's

beer and stepped away from the door to lean against the wall, trying to catch her breath.

"What's nice? The cue or the beer?"

"Both." She inhaled and exhaled, her breathing calming, her heart still racing. "Beer first."

"You've got blood on you."

Sarah looked down and saw a sprinkle of Adam DePont's blood on her arm. She shrugged. "Don't we all?" She smiled. The woman didn't. "Sure looks like blood, eh?" She moved away from the door. "Lunch break from my paint job." She spoke in a matter-of-fact voice, the kind that usually wasn't challenged. Footsteps pounded the pavement outside. She ignored it, and no one tried to yank open the door. "How about that beer?"

The woman turned and shouted, "Hey, Debbie? Need another beer over here. Just bring what I'm drinking."

The woman behind the bar nodded and opened the fridge.

"My name's Teresa. And you are?" Teresa set her beer down and proffered her hand.

Sarah walked away from the wall, shook it, and looked back at the door. No one was there. She turned back to Teresa and said, "I'm Sarah."

"So, Sarah, a game of pool?"

"Sure."

Teresa pointed at the wall. "Grab a cue. I'll rack 'em."

The beer came, and they played pool like old friends. Teresa was quite good, Sarah unpracticed. She made small errors on angles, not using enough backspin on the side pocket, and sunk the cue ball a couple of times.

After two games and one beer, Sarah needed to leave. The woman behind the bar had come over to watch them play.

"So soon," Debbie asked.

"I have some things I need to take care of."

"We understand," Teresa said. She set her cue on the felt of the nearest table and embraced Sarah.

Sarah frowned, not used to the affection. Then Debbie hugged her.

"Anything you can tell us?" Teresa asked.

They knew who she was. Of course, they did. Why wouldn't they? Sarah's face had been all over the news.

"All this time …" Sarah paused. "You knew me?"

Teresa nodded, exchanged a knowing glance with Debbie, and then looked back at Sarah.

"You're not here for either one of us?" Debbie asked. "To change our future? No message from beyond?"

Sarah shook her head. "Sadly, no. Nothing like that."

"Then why our pool hall?" Teresa asked.

"It was completely random. I was being pursued."

"Well, then." Teresa held up her beer in a toast. "We're glad to have offered you refuge and had the chance to play pool with you."

"Me too."

"Us girls need to stick together, Sarah."

Sarah started for the door.

"Just in case you ever have a message for either of us, my name is Teresa Wiitanen, and this is Debbie Clanton. We own this place. Come back any time and play pool. Drink with us. Think of it as a place of refuge. We'll close anytime to have you to ourselves."

Sarah reached the door and peeked outside. The street was busy, but no one waited for her.

She turned back to the two women. "I do have a message for you both."

That got their attention. Debbie leaned forward, followed by Teresa.

"I'm to thank you for your hospitality and tell you to never change. Kindhearted people like you two'll make this world a better place."

"Sarah, you're mistaken. You're making the world a better place. Now go, do your thing before we kidnap you and keep you all to ourselves."

She smiled and nodded respectfully to them. They returned the nod.

Then she unlocked the door, stepped outside in the late afternoon wind, and started north on Yonge Street, the ball cap pulled low.

Her ride to the north was waiting. She had no idea where she was going yet or why, but she was pretty sure it had something to do with the man who had called her that morning.

Vivian would tell her more soon.

All she had to do was get to the Toronto public library north of Bloor Street and go to the study tables on the second floor. A woman named Echo Bos was waiting for her but didn't know it yet. Echo was visiting Toronto from the States, had a rental car, and was researching Sarah at the library.

A chance at a personal interview in exchange for a two-hour ride north was not out of the question.

Sarah would even buy dinner.

The word *Blacken* rippled through her thoughts again.

By the time she reached the library and was on the stairs heading to her meeting with Echo, Vivian told her the rest, including what had happened to Kymberly Blacken.

Sarah stopped halfway up the stairs, her grip tightening on the railing.

"But they're married," she whispered out loud. "How could he be so cruel?"

Vivian sounded concerned. Kymberly was locked up and had been there a considerable time without food or water. Meet Echo Bos, get in the car, and arrive by midnight.

After that, it would all work out.

Everything would work out.

Or so Vivian thought.

Sarah continued up the stairs, a chill coursing through her.

Chapter 33

PARKMAN FINISHED WITH THE rental gear, securing it in the boat. Once that was all loaded and the trailer was secure, they went to dinner at a roadside diner near Huntsville, Ontario.

Both men ordered but didn't eat much, only picking at their meals.

"Man, this is hard, Parkman."

He regarded Aaron with a fatherly eye. "Aaron, you know what's hard?"

"What?"

"The slow period before the action. The anticipation of what's around the corner." He sat back in his chair and fiddled with a toothpick in his mouth. "Think about it this way. It's like going to court. The day or two before, the nerves are high, blood pressure's high, but when you get to court, it's over pretty quickly. And, if the judgment goes in your favor, you might wonder what all the nerves were about. That's this. That's what I'm feeling right now."

Aaron nodded, set down his fork, and pushed his plate forward. "I can't eat anymore. I feel sick for her."

"Me too, Aaron. She'll be fine, though. She always is. We just feel aimless as we prepare to meet her, prepare to deal with whatever's coming tonight or tomorrow morning. It's turning my stomach, too."

He glanced around the half-empty restaurant. No one paid them any attention. They were alone in their corner. Even the waitress only came over twice. Once to take their order and once to deliver it.

"And to know she'll be unconscious, underwater," Aaron said. "I mean, what the fuck? Why does she willingly walk into these situations?"

"You know why. She wouldn't be Sarah if she didn't."

Aaron snatched his fork off the table, picked at the over-boiled vegetables, then set his fork back down. He checked his watch. "Six more hours until we're supposed to be in the woods behind some cabin. Looking for what, exactly?"

Parkman shrugged. "No idea. But we follow Sarah's rules. No weapons. No cell phones. She was pretty sure she'd be in a lot of danger if we brought a weapon or a cell phone."

"Yeah, they track cell phones. If we got pulled over and caught with weapons, we couldn't be there for her when she needed us."

"That's right. Remember, she told us not to speed, either. Attract no attention whatsoever. Just be there at all costs, and everything will work out."

"I know." Aaron leaned forward and placed his elbows on the table. "It's good to talk it out, hear it all again. Clears the jumble of emotions in my head." He grunted. "I just cannot wait for this to be over."

Parkman shoved his plate away. "You have no idea, my friend. Me too." He spit the toothpick out and grabbed a new one. "I was supposed to be home by now. But it seems I've been working with Sarah for so many years, it's all I know how to do." He caught the waitress's eye and gestured for her to come over. "And I love every minute I can help Sarah. She's my world. Of course, in a non-intimate way."

"I know, Parkman. You have no idea how grateful I am. Without you, I don't know what would've happened to Sarah over the years."

The waitress asked if the food was okay.

"We thought we were hungrier than we actually were," Parkman said. "Can you bring us coffee and the bill?"

The waitress fumbled with the dishes and dropped one of the forks.

"I'm sorry," she said, stooping to pick it up. Once she'd retrieved the fork, she continued to collect their dishes, cleared her throat loudly, and stepped away from the table.

"What the hell was that all about?" Aaron asked when she was out of earshot.

"I don't know, but I don't think we should stick around for the coffee. We can go to a drive-thru on the way north."

"Agreed. Should we just bail?"

Parkman shook his head. "I'd love to leave now. But running out on the bill will attract unnecessary attention."

Aaron pulled out two twenties. "That'll easily cover our

meal."

"True. Let's go."

The chairs screeched as they pushed them back in unison.

The front door opened at the same time, and two uniformed Ontario Provincial Police officers entered.

Parkman hesitated.

"Act normal," he whispered. "We have no idea if they're here for us."

Both officers scanned the restaurant, and eventually, their eyes landed on Parkman and Aaron.

"Scratch that. They're here for us."

"Fuck." Aaron sounded angry. "We can't be taken in, Parkman," he whispered. "Sarah dies without us."

"I know. Just be ready."

"I'm always ready."

One officer stepped forward. "Aaron Stevens," he said. "We'd like to have a word with you. And you look like Parkman. Is that correct?"

Parkman nodded. "There a problem, Officer?"

Parkman and Aaron were still by their table, the officers barely inside the restaurant's front door. The other diners remained silent, the place suddenly as quiet as four in the morning. The traffic noise outside had stopped as well.

Did they block the highway?

"There's no problem, Parkman. We just have a couple of questions regarding the whereabouts of a Sarah Roberts."

"We have no idea where Sarah might be." Which was completely true.

"Still, we'd like to have this discussion at our

detachment. You have an hour or two to spare?"

"Uh," Parkman glanced at Aaron, then back at the officers. "We're kinda busy, guys. The boating trip is planned and all. How about tomorrow or the day after? We'll drop in on our way south."

The officers exchanged a glance and moved a few steps closer.

"Parkman, I understand you used to be one of us."

Parkman nodded.

"Then you know how this works. We're going to head in and have a chat. Neither of you are under arrest at this time. We are asking you to come willingly. But if you refuse, we will be forced to arrest you both. Is that clear?"

Parkman stared him down. These men were standing in the way of them helping Sarah. Cops or not, they could not allow themselves to go with the OPP.

"Aaron," he whispered without moving his lips. "Can you take them both down quickly, without trouble?"

"Yes," came the confident reply.

"Follow my lead."

"What's that?" the cop asked. "What're you two saying?"

"We were deciding if you're a real cop," Parkman said. "We've had trouble in the past with men posing as cops. You have badges, I presume? Let's see 'em."

Both officers looked mildly irritated. Parkman was getting under their skin in front of an audience of about ten other diners.

Just wait. The show they'd put on for the diners would be epic.

He started forward and whispered to Aaron, "For Sarah."

"For Sarah," Aaron whispered back, following Parkman to the cops near the front door.

Chapter 34

NEAR THE RESEARCH TABLES in the Toronto Public Library, Sarah grabbed a large book on Greece, a country she'd visited, and sat beside Echo. She opened the book and browsed the scenes. They had plenty of time to get to know one another. She didn't need to be up north until around midnight, and it was only six in the evening.

It had been a long day and would be a long night and day tomorrow, so she enjoyed the calm, relaxing atmosphere of the library.

Echo scanned a pile of newspapers, a pen, and a pad of paper beside her. After a minute, while Sarah examined pictures of Athens, Echo moved papers aside and started on other documents.

"Excuse me," Sarah whispered. "What're you

researching?"

Echo glanced over, looked away, then mumbled, "Just something I find fascinating—" She stopped suddenly, then slowly turned back to Sarah. When her eyes locked on Sarah, she jumped in her seat and almost lost her balance. "Sarah? Sarah Roberts?"

"I thought I'd come to join you and have a chat." She leaned closer. "You know, one on one."

Echo's mouth fell open. She gasped, her stare incredulous. "But, how did you know—"

"Really?" She arched her eyebrows high. "Echo, I know a lot about you."

Echo Bos blanched.

"You're in Toronto visiting friends. You know I spend a lot of time in Toronto because it's Aaron's home. You're from Duluth, Minnesota. You hate liars and onions, and your middle name is Nicole—your dad called you Nick, though. You and your husband Lee have a beautiful daughter named …" Sarah paused a moment, waiting for Vivian to give her the name. She looked skyward, then said, "She does have a daughter, right?" She raised a finger for Echo to stay quiet and not supply the answer.

After a moment, Sarah nodded. "Right, okay." She looked at Echo and said, "Abigail. How am I doing so far?"

Echo's shaky fingers touched her lips for a brief moment, then dropped to touch her throat.

"I'm just …"

"Just," Sarah prodded. "Go ahead."

"Just shocked to see you. Then hear all that." She gulped audibly. "It's a bit overwhelming."

Sarah nodded. "Sorry. I wanted to break the ice. You hate liars, so I wanted you to know I'm on the up and up."

"I know how you look. I mean, I've seen your picture. Hey, wait," she looked around the library conspiratorially, "aren't they looking for you right now?"

Sarah closed the Greece book and leaned in close. "They are, and you're going to help me evade the police. Can I rely on you?"

Her face colored again, the pale, giving way to a red blush.

"You mean, like in aiding and abetting?"

"Yes, but there's risk involved. You could get caught."

"I've never been a *bad* girl like that. I'm in. What do I have to do?"

"Smuggle me out of Toronto in your car."

Her eyes widened. "Like in my trunk?"

"No, I'll sit up front. We can talk on the way. But I need to get out of the city, and I have no one who'll take me without spilling the beans. Would you do it?"

After scanning the immediate area again, Echo leaned in to Sarah and said, "Of course. When should we go?"

"As soon as you're ready."

"Now."

"I need you to take me two hours north of here."

"No issue. I'll just call my husband when I get to the car —"

"No calls," Sarah said, her voice stern.

"Right. Of course. No calls." She fished out her cell phone from her purse and held it up. "Turning it off now."

"There's no risk to you, Echo. You can call Lee when I'm

out of your car, but you can't talk about me to anyone for at least two days. Can you do that?"

"Absolutely."

Sarah reached out her hand. "Then we have a deal."

Echo shook Sarah's hand. "Deal."

They got up at the same time and headed for the front doors.

Sarah had secured her ride north—as Vivian had promised.

The day had been difficult. The evening would be worse. Mostly because Vivian wasn't talking about what to expect on a rural road off Highway 11 in northern Ontario cottage country.

Sarah was just supposed to be there after midnight, and Vivian would direct her from there.

The story of my life ...

Chapter 35

PARKMAN EXAMINED THE COPS' IDs, both of them checking out.

"How long will this take?" Parkman asked.

"An hour, maybe two."

"What's it regarding?"

The cop focused his attention on Aaron. "We have reason to believe that Sarah Roberts planted a device on the prison bus to take out its brakes."

Aaron moved closer. "She would never do that."

"After a short pursuit, investigating officers located the car you and Sarah had rented at a Kingston agency."

Aaron nodded. "That's where we dropped it off. Still no evidence to support your claim."

"Inside the rental, which hadn't been readied for anyone

else when our team got to it, they located a gas receipt scrunched up in the back seat of the car with *thirteen dead* written on it in Sarah's handwriting."

"That's all you got?" Aaron laughed. "Doesn't mean either of us crawled under that bus and did anything to it. If she wrote it down and you can prove it was her handwriting, then she did so after we saw the accident."

"Either way, let's continue this at our office."

"Okay," Parkman said and stepped to the side, getting himself closer to the second officer. "Aaron, you okay with heading in for a chat with these guys?"

Aaron moved forward like he walked on a cloud, all light and graceful. "No, not really. Free country and all. Unless we're being arrested, we're not going anywhere with anyone for any reason. And I'm not being arrested today." He shook his head. "Not today."

The officers responded to the tension in the air. The cop in front reached for his pepper spray, the one behind, his cuffs on the duty belt.

Aaron slipped inside the first officer's space and did something quickly to the man's throat. Without a sound, he collapsed to the restaurant floor in a heap, a gasp from someone in the restaurant the only sound.

Parkman was already on the second cop, shoving his cuff arm back and spinning him around, off balance. They stepped back together, Parkman keeping the cop off balance, unable to right himself and gain control of the situation.

Aaron hopped over to them, wrapped an arm around the second cop, and cut off his airflow while Parkman held his arms back.

"Hey," a customer bellowed. "You can't do that."

"Fuck off," Parkman shouted. "Interfere at your own risk."

The average person didn't have the balls to challenge someone in a fight, leaving Parkman pretty confident no one would try to stop them.

In a matter of seconds, both officers were asleep on the floor of the small diner.

Parkman ran to the front window. "Shit," he said. "Their cruiser's blocking us in."

He looked back as Aaron snatched the keys off the lead cop's outer belt. He grabbed one of their radios as well.

Good thinking.

Parkman ran for the rental car with the boat trailer while Aaron jumped in the cruiser. Once inside the rental, his heart in his throat at what they had just done and the eventual consequences, Parkman got the car in gear and checked his mirrors.

Aaron reversed the cruiser out of the way, then hit the highway and sped off.

"What the hell?" Parkman asked out loud. "He's stealing the cop car, too?"

Then he noticed what had spooked Aaron. Even as Parkman hit the gas, everyone from inside the diner wanted to be a hero now—even the waitress. Two diners held up cell phones, probably recording what Parkman looked like, the vehicle make and model. There was no time for Aaron to park the cruiser and then jump in the rental with Parkman. They needed out of there immediately.

Parkman hit the highway with only a quick glimpse at

the road before merging onto it. Luckily, no one was coming, and he fell in behind the cruiser, which was over a hundred meters ahead of him.

"Shit, shit, shit."

After about five kilometers, Aaron signaled to leave the highway. Parkman followed.

Once they were far enough away from the highway, Aaron pulled onto a dirt road, stopped on the shoulder, and cut the engine. Parkman pulled in behind the stolen cruiser.

Aaron jumped in the passenger seat.

"Holy shit, Parkman," he said upon slamming the door. "What did we just do?"

"Yeah, I know. Something to think about. But not now. Tomorrow. Think about it tomorrow." Parkman continued along the dirt road, looking for a place to turn around. "We have to get as far away from that cruiser as possible. They track them with GPS."

"And those diners saw this car and boat."

"I know."

"What do we do now? We still have about a thirty-minute drive." He tapped the dash by the clock. "And we have to be on that rural road in three hours."

"I have no idea, Aaron. I have no idea."

Parkman finally reached a grassy area big enough to turn the car and trailer around. He managed to do it without having to reverse and started back down the dirt road.

Moments later, they passed the parked cruiser and continued toward the highway.

"This safe?" Aaron asked. "Heading back to the highway?"

"No."

"Shit."

"I wish we still had our cell phones. We could check for an alternate route."

"Stop!" Aaron shouted.

Parkman jammed on the brakes, shoving him forward into the steering wheel. Aaron braced himself on the dash.

Then he jumped from the car and sprinted back to the parked cruiser. Parkman watched through the rearview mirror, the interior light of the cruiser shining on Aaron's head and shoulders. Parkman waited as the clock ticked dangerously close to two minutes.

"C'mon, Aaron. What're you doing?"

It had to be at least four minutes before Aaron popped back out of the cruiser, slammed the door, and ran back.

He hopped back in the front seat. "Hit it," he said.

Parkman jammed the gas pedal downward. "What was that all about?"

"Their computer was logged on, so I didn't need the password."

"And?" The sign for the highway was coming up on the right.

"I was able to bring up a map."

"Good news?" Parkman asked as he slowed to take the turn back onto the highway.

"We're five minutes from Huntsville. There's an exit we can take that'll get us off the highway. We can get where we want to go without returning onto this highway."

"Good thinking."

"Thanks."

Parkman fished a toothpick from his pocket and placed it on his lips.

"They have nothing with that gas receipt business," he said.

"Not for conviction," Aaron added. "But enough to want to talk to us."

"Yeah. True."

Aaron turned on the cop's radio he'd snagged. A female dispatcher radioed calls to several units. Parkman paid attention to calls for the diner. Backup was called in for officers down.

Minutes later, the description of the suspects' vehicle and boat trailer came over the cop's radio. The plate number was incomplete.

They rode in silence and listened to the dispatcher until the exit. Parkman was convinced if they encountered the police again that night, it would not end well. They had to be there for Sarah. The police would hamper that goal, and Parkman and Aaron couldn't allow that. The police would resort to force.

Deadly force.

Parkman drove on through the night, anxiety building in his stomach. He didn't want to die.

He'd have no choice but to run from the cops.

No choice at all.

Not running from the cops meant Sarah would die.

Chapter 36

Sarah and Echo chatted the entire way about Echo's life, her husband, and her daughter. Sarah talked a little about her life, satisfying Echo's curiosity.

When they stopped for coffee, Echo parked in a darkened area of the large lot and walked in to get them coffee and something to eat, keeping Sarah secluded from public view.

Sarah was happy for the company, the calm. She hadn't heard from Vivian since the library, but it didn't matter. She knew the turnoff—or at least she would know it when they got there.

The signs for Huntsville came and went. Several police cruisers raced by in the other direction, rooftop lights on.

"I wonder what's going on," Echo said.

A knot formed in the pit of Sarah's stomach. "Me too."

"Can't Vivian just tell you?"

"It doesn't work like that. Vivian only tells me something with a purpose. Something I can use or act on. Random police chases or even if they're searching for a robbery suspect, whatever it may be, has nothing to do with me unless Vivian makes it my business." She glanced at Echo. "My sister sees the big picture. Even when I'm dealing with something that doesn't make sense to me, I go on blind trust, and it always seems to work out."

"That is a lot of trust." Echo opened a pack of gum and offered Sarah one. Sarah declined, and then Echo popped a piece in her mouth. Around the gum, she said, "Has Vivian ever made a mistake, led you astray?"

Sarah laughed. "I'd say yes. Vivian would say no."

"Interesting." A wide smile played across Echo's lips. "Sisters fight. Do you two? I mean, wouldn't that be cool? The dead sister and the one still alive, at each other's throats —" Her face soured, and she snatched a glimpse at Sarah. "Sorry, that was insensitive."

"It's okay. I can't be offended. There was no intent. And yes, we fight. I've called her out, called her names, and swore every horrid word I know at her in the past."

"Lovely."

Sarah sipped the last bit of her coffee and set the empty cup in the cup holder. "Yeah, I guess you could call it that."

They were getting close.

"We're almost there," Sarah said, leaning forward in her seat. "I can feel it."

Two more OPP cruisers raced by the other way, lights ablaze.

Vivian? What's going on? Related to me?

Nothing came back. She was on her own. Her ability to lock in where she was going honed after years of working with her sister.

"Maybe five more minutes, Echo."

"No issue. Wherever, whenever. I'm loving our chat. I don't want to drop you off."

"Remember your promise. Two days. Then just tell your husband. If the authorities get wind you drove me up here, you could be charged with something because they're looking for me, and you helped me."

"It'll be our little secret. You, me, and Lee."

"Thank you."

She touched Echo's shoulder, squeezed gently, then brought her attention back to the road ahead.

"Turn at the next exit."

Echo slowed. Minutes later, they were navigating a side road, then another. Finally, she had Echo turn down a road that was a dead end and had her stop on the shoulder.

"I can't let you out here," Echo whispered.

"Why not?"

"It's pitch black." She looked at Sarah. "And spooky. How will you see where you're going? How will you get home?"

"I have friends coming to pick me up." She tapped Echo's shoulder again. "Don't worry about me. I can use the light of the moon to walk the road. I'm good."

"Are you sure?"

Sarah nodded. "Can you find the highway again? We just did a couple of crazy turns."

"I've got GPS. We're good."

"I can't thank you enough for the ride."

"It was my pleasure."

They embraced as best they could in the front seat, said their goodbyes, and Sarah exited the vehicle.

She stood on the side of the road as Echo turned around and sped off.

Then Sarah jogged down into the ditch and was lost in the gloom of the trees.

Chapter 37

BLACKEN COULDN'T SLEEP. HE'D passed out earlier after his shots of bourbon, then woke suddenly at sirens in the distance. Out on his front porch, the sirens faded.

He came back in and tried to sleep but couldn't. Now, it was almost midnight, and he was wide awake. And sober.

He made a cup of tea and sat out on the veranda. He would watch the stars in the dark and listen for any vehicles approaching. The sirens earlier unsettled him. He usually couldn't hear that sort of thing this far from the highway.

Feet up, he stared at the stars and wondered how it would all play out. Jail was a real possibility for him when court dates could be secured a year down the road. His lawyers would argue that he should remain free before trial. Cops never fared well in prison.

Or he could erase all the evidence linking him to any crimes. Completely destroy anything they could trace back to him. If he could get a hold of Sarah—that plan died along with Russell's withdrawal from his tasks—then maybe he could blame her for his ex-wife's death.

Either way, the ex would be dead within a day or two, and then he could hunt down Jensen. Once Jensen was dead, Blacken would figure something else out for himself.

He would hide until his plan was foolproof, and he'd never be convicted on any charge in any court.

But was that possible?

Forensics would easily prove Blacken was a prisoner in Jensen's basement. He'd left DNA onsite. Kymberly's DNA in the cabin made sense—it was her cabin as much as his.

The two mafia goons in Jensen's home—one dead and one severely beaten—spoke more about the friends Jensen kept than what happened to them when a decorated detective was escaping with his life.

He could spin the tale better than O.J. and would walk away without their charges sticking—no glove needed.

As for the ex-wife: no body, no case.

For all they knew, she ran away when she was caught cheating with Jensen. He'd subpoena his private investigator, who kept the original photos of Jensen and Kymberly in bed.

He sipped his tea and realized he could even cast suspicion of Kymberly's demise onto Jensen. What did Jensen do to her when the affair was discovered?

Something moved in the bush at the side of the house.

Blacken froze and listened. His gun was inside. He wasn't expecting any visitors.

He waited for several heartbeats, and when the noise didn't repeat, he turned slowly and looked into the darkness where the tree line started at the edge of his property.

Nothing moved.

Probably a moose, or maybe something smaller like a fox or a coyote.

He brought the tea to his lips, sipped silently, and listened.

An owl hooted in the distance. He swore he heard a police siren somewhere, but that could've been his mind playing tricks. He'd heard sirens every day for decades. Almost absolute silence often brought mind-created phantom sounds to life. Like walking through an empty house and hearing a creak or a howl. No one was there. The windows were closed, but the mind enjoyed its tricks.

He set down his teacup and got to his feet. Better to get inside and lock the doors on the off chance someone was out there, watching him.

One step, two steps, and he was back in front of the door.

Then he heard something new. A scratching sound from inside the house.

The ex-wife. Trying to get out. Crying and screaming, the sound muffled so much that he couldn't hear it until he was standing in front of the open screen door of the cabin.

"Fuck me," he whispered. "Spooking the shit out of myself."

He stepped inside and was about to close the door when he was sure he heard a car engine.

The door stopped an inch from closing.

He waited, breathing in and out slowly, listening. After a

moment, he opened the door wide and peered out the screen again.

The dirt road in front of the cabin was empty. No headlights, no vehicles, nothing.

He shook his head.

"Hearing things," he muttered under his breath, then closed the door and locked it.

Chapter 38

SARAH WATCHED THE MAN on his front porch, sipping from a coffee mug. She stood in the woods, several trees back from where the grass of the cabin's yard had started.

According to Vivian, this was the house. The man on the porch was Joel Blacken, although he didn't look too scary to her.

Beware of The Blacken.

What the hell was that supposed to mean? Blacken had to be in his fifties, with a slight bulge in the abdomen and possibly an insomniac. He sat out watching the sky as Sarah watched him. Nothing unusual at all. Why was he so scary? What had he done?

Vivian had disappeared again.

Kymberly Blacken was inside the cabin, locked in a hole

in the cabin's cellar. That was enough for her to enter the cabin and hurt Blacken.

While Sarah watched Blacken on his porch, she was sure she heard a police siren in the distance. Just as Blacken entered his cabin, the crunch of gravel under a tire and the soft purr of a car engine drifted to her, but then it was gone.

Could Parkman and Aaron be showing up early? Her two-part note for them was to nab her at this location close to one in the morning. If they miss her, then they know what to do around sunrise. And at the sight of a weapon, Sarah had instructed them to go to plan B.

She leaned against a tree, and a twig moved underfoot. Leaves slipped to the side, and Blacken stopped moving. As she watched him, he slowly looked directly at her. She was too well hidden to be seen in the dark.

Evidently, whatever he was up to, he was paranoid and listening to everything.

She would have to approach the house stealthily to get inside without Blacken knowing. Once she obtained the upper hand, Blacken would tell her everything she wanted to know under threat of extreme pain.

When Parkman and Aaron arrived, they would learn everything they needed to know. If Blacken was involved in the murder of those prisoners bound for Milhaven, he would stand trial, and Sarah would be cleared.

In a perfect world, that was how it should go down, but nothing ever played out the way it was planned.

Even so, she had to try.

Everything related to the man in the cabin. As far as she could tell, Blacken was alone—except for his wife. One vehicle was on the property, and one man was on the veranda with the lights off inside the cabin.

Sarah silently edged forward, leaning against the trees as she made slow progress, testing each step so she didn't make a noise or lose her balance. She stopped and waited when she was directly behind the house, calming her breath.

To rest, she sat on a fallen tree, elbows on her thighs, and watched the house. She must've sat like that for at least thirty minutes, which would have given Parkman and Aaron time to get closer in place.

In that time, she could've sworn she heard police sirens at least twice more.

What could possibly be causing such an uproar of activity in northern Ontario? It's not like they were downtown Toronto, where she would hear sirens a dozen times or more on some Friday nights.

It couldn't be about her as she had anonymously arrived at Blacken's cabin. Even Echo Bos had no idea where she was now. After leaving Sarah on that side road, Sarah walked over four kilometers in the dark to get to the right area. That's too large a space to search in a short time if Echo had been pulled over and questioned.

Something about Echo comforted Sarah. Just like the women in the pool hall and Lacee back at the motel café— none of them would rat Sarah out very easily. She was sure of it.

At least thirty minutes had passed when Sarah decided to advance on the cabin. That meant walking into the open. She waited, ready, at the edge of the trees, staring at the cabin's windows, then stepped out into the open. She took another step, prepared to jump back into cover at the sight of danger or a light flicking on.

Six feet from the trees, she edged a little to the right to head toward the area between two windows at the back of the cabin's wall.

No cameras were visible. No red lights flashed anywhere.

Yet her nerves registered danger.

Vivian, where are you? This is the right move, no?

She took another step, then checked behind her. Then, another step.

A sound to her left startled her. She lowered her body, hands up. Nothing there.

She exhaled deeply, righted herself, then stepped closer to the cabin—and dropped.

One second, she was on the grass, the next, falling under it.

A large tarp gave way, and she fell into a dark hole. The black maw opened, and she had no idea how deep it was. But then she stopped falling, so suddenly her left ankle collapsed to the side under her weight.

She squealed in pain, then clamped a hand over her mouth, but it was too late. If Blacken didn't know she was there before, he certainly did now.

She felt her way around the hole and got to the earthy wall. After getting herself into position, her teeth clenched at the pain in her ankle, she got to her good foot and searched for something to lift herself up and out of the hole. But there was nothing. The top of the hole was slightly above her head, the edges fragile, dirt crumbling away in her grasp.

A door shut loudly from somewhere above.

Blacken was coming.

He laid a trap, and she'd fallen right into it.

Thanks, Vivian. Could've used your help here.

Thinking back to her conversation with Echo, this was a moment to curse her sister. Where was she when she needed her most? Why hadn't she warned her about the large *fucking* hole in the ground?

Sarah lowered herself in the dark and put her back to the corner of the hole, taking all weight off her bad ankle.

Light flashed across the top. Someone came closer, exercising caution.

"Hello?" a man called.

Sarah waited.

"Is someone there?" he asked.

The bright flashlight beamed down into her face. She raised a hand to ward off the light.

"Well, hello there, Sarah. What a pleasure to see you here. I wasn't expecting you."

"Can you turn that thing off?"

"Carrying any weapons on you, Sarah?"

She shot her hands out to the side, then patted her pants. "None. Now, turn that off or at least shine it somewhere else."

The light moved to the side.

"I thought I heard something earlier," Blacken said. "That was you in the trees when I was out having tea."

Sarah didn't respond. She gripped her already swelling ankle and massaged it. A twist, possibly a sprain, but nothing seemed broken, which was good. She'd had a broken foot before and hated it.

"I imagine you want out?" Blacken asked.

"Yeah, and some ice."

"Sure thing, Sarah. I'll go get the ladder."

Blacken and the flashlight disappeared. There was something in his tone that didn't sit well with her. Something in his demeanor.

She had been warned about Blacken and would be extra vigilant, extra cautious around him. She still had no idea what role he played in what had been happening over the past few days.

She held her swelling ankle, breathed through her teeth to control the pain, and waited to see what would happen. Vivian had disappeared.

Again.

It was as if Vivian had betrayed her. Set her up to become Blacken's prisoner.

Could her sister be the one responsible for the *vile betrayal*?

Sarah shook her head to clear that thought because if that was the case, Sarah was as good as dead.

Chapter 39

Blacken returned several minutes later. He dropped something heavy, out of sight, by the edge of the hole. Sarah waited, the night sky offering minimal light to see.

He was doing something a few feet from the hole's edge, her stomach knotting up with each second he didn't appear.

What the fuck? Vivian?

Finally, he glanced over the edge. "You ready to come up and nurse that foot?"

She didn't respond.

"I've brought the ladder."

She waited.

"Can you climb on one foot?"

She nodded, wondering if he could see the gesture in the dark.

"With a blindfold?" He tossed something down to her.

A balaclava. Just like the gang members at the motel.

"Put it on over your head backward."

"Why? I've already seen the house. I was in the woods, remember?"

"Fine. But it was at night. I'm bringing you up from the hole where I will take you into my home. I will call an ambulance to have them swing by, look at your foot, and take you to town. The less detail you remember, the better for me."

He was lying. There was no ambulance in her future. She didn't need Vivian to know that.

"Seriously," she said, not interested in games. "What's the blindfold for?"

He waited a heartbeat, then said, "It's the price of the ladder. Put it on, and you can come out. Leave it off, and fuck you. I walk away. I'll check back in a week or two." He shrugged. "I couldn't care less."

"Just say that next time," she muttered under her breath.

"What's that?"

She reached for the balaclava. "Same shit, different day. Bigger pile, more flies." After slipping it on her head, she waited, the night now a rich dark black. She could see nothing at all. It wouldn't be easy to tear off, either.

The distinctive sound of aluminum being maneuvered into place came from her right. She waited until he was finished, then listened for further movement. For all she knew, he could be climbing down into the hole with her.

"Sarah?"

She tilted her head toward the sound. "What?"

"The ladder's in place. Come out slowly. No tricks."

She eased up to her one good foot and hopped to the dirt wall, feeling around for the ladder. She hopped again, leaning forward, moving along the wall, hands first.

"Two more feet," Blacken said.

She hopped once more, her hand bumping the side of the ladder. After getting into position by feel, she clung to its sides and jumped up onto the first step. She repeated the move until she was halfway up the ladder.

"Well done, Sarah. And in the dark, no less. A couple more steps, and you'll be high enough to get off the ladder."

She jumped two more times, then leaned forward, feeling the grass. If she edged around the side of the ladder, she could plop onto the lawn.

Blacken's hand clamped down on her right wrist. "Here, I'll guide you."

She jerked her hand out of his grasp in one swift movement.

"I can do it myself."

"Temper, temper."

She detected him moving back, giving her room.

Sarah pivoted on the rung, her calf muscle protesting from holding her weight. When she felt she was ready and had a good idea of where the ground was, she thrust her butt out toward it and lifted off the ladder rung.

For a moment, she was suspended in the air. Then she dropped onto her rump so hard it rattled her teeth.

But she was out of the hole.

Blacken's hands slipped under her shoulders and lifted her upward. She grunted and stepped on her good foot, so she didn't bump her twisted ankle.

When she was standing, with his help, he tried to spin her toward him. His clumsy hands, lack of proper balance, and inability to compensate for her weight made him stagger backward.

Sarah hopped twice, then lost her balance, a small yip escaping as she tumbled toward him. One moment, he was there, clinging to her, then he was gone, and she was falling. With her hands out to break her fall, the ground came quickly.

Even though she couldn't see a thing, her eyes clenched shut, and her face tightened for impact.

Pain made her angry. It always had. When she shuddered to the ground, she landed partially on top of him, bumping her swollen ankle in the process.

She screamed out, hands clenching into fists.

He squirmed under her with a high-pitched grunt.

She didn't wait for him to move again, to get out from under her. Aaron had spent several sessions a few years back training her to fight blindfolded. You never knew when someone threw sand in your eyes, and you had to focus on your other senses to repel an attack.

Sarah rolled her weight onto him and began to pummel his face, getting a couple of good shots into his jaw and mouth.

Nearly spent, she rolled off and away from the hole in the ground, got to her knees, and ripped off the balaclava.

Sarah gasped out loud. "What did you do?" she shouted, unsure if she was asking herself or Blacken that question.

He stood several feet away with a flashlight and a cell

phone. The light shone on a woman lying near the hole where the ladder still stuck out. Dark splotches on her face could be blood. Her mouth open, eyes closed, the woman looked beat up and unconscious.

"What have you done?" Sarah asked, her tone hard, serious.

Blacken let out a short laugh. Whatever he'd done, he found it quite amusing. After clicking something on the phone, he lowered it and stared at her.

"You came out of the hole on your own. When I tried to help you, you rebuffed my help, knocked me out of the way, and landed on my ex-wife. You beat the shit out of her, Sarah. I've got you on video attacking a defenseless woman."

"You set it up. You made me wear the blindfold so I wouldn't see it was her. I felt you lose your balance, but you didn't, did you? It was planned so I would land on her and think it's you—"

"Think what you want, Sarah. I've got you on camera. You're guilty. And when they find your body alongside hers, everyone will know you lost your fucking mind." He dropped the cell phone into his front pocket. From behind his back, Blacken produced a weapon with a sound suppressor. "Get up. Hop, jump, skip, or walk. I don't fucking care. But get up and get inside that house."

She leveled her gaze at him, adrenaline pumping her heart into her throat. Everything in her being wanted to get up and smash his face into a dented chunk of bloody watermelon.

"And if I don't?" she asked, her voice steely.

"I will shoot you where you sit, roll your body into that

hole, add my ex-wife into it, too, then fill it in. One day, when someone buys this cabin and wants to perform renovations, they'll locate bones in the backyard. I've already reported my ex-wife as a missing person. It'll be quite easy to add your name to the hundreds of girls who go missing every year."

He stepped closer, the tip of the weapon an ominous reminder of how close she seemed to death daily without Vivian there to get her out of it.

And no warning on where to walk to avoid large fucking holes in the ground. But no, Vivian only came when convenient for her and not Sarah.

"I'll get up. But only because you do have a compelling argument. I wouldn't want to ruin a renovation. Bones prompt investigations."

The edge of his mouth turned upward in a smirk. "Haven't lost your sense of humor. Even when a gun's pointed at you."

She turned onto her knees, then lifted up gingerly. "If you knew how many times a gun was pointed at me, you'd be surprised I still have my senses at all, let alone humor."

"Okay, enough talk. Move. Toward the house."

Sarah stared at him a moment longer, listening to the intense quiet around them, then glanced at the cabin.

"Front door or back?"

"Back."

She hopped toward the back door, wondering if Parkman and Aaron were watching.

This house was the first one on their list. She'd given them the best directions she could after Vivian gave them to her. They were to follow the same route she had followed.

But there was one problem.

Since she had told them not to carry weapons, they were also told if they saw weapons at the cabin to back off and not attempt a rescue. Blacken aimed at Sarah. He followed her at a distance as she walked across the lawn toward the cabin's back door. If Parkman and Aaron were watching, they would leave. Clear instructions: under no circumstances were they to approach her or the cabin if they saw or heard a weapon.

She glanced to her right to stare at the thick darkness of the tree line. Then to her left.

At the door, Blacken reached around her and pushed it open.

"Inside."

After one last look at the woods, Sarah stepped inside and lost all hope for rescue.

Chapter 40

Blacken followed Sarah up the steps and into the small kitchen. It had been easy to grab his ex-wife and bring her outside. Drowsy from lack of food and sleep and in a weakened state, she was able to exit the basement with only a little help and the promise of food. Once upstairs, he'd smashed her in the head with the butt of his gun until her eyes rolled back and she was out.

Something about that felt good. There had been many times throughout their marriage when he wanted to smash the butt of his gun into her teeth but found a reserve of inner strength to resist. *One day,* he told himself. *One day ...*

Then, she began cheating on him. Routinely. The ungrateful bitch opened her legs for other men while he was out risking his life in the line of duty, often coming home bruised because a jacked-up druggie decided to go berserk on the cops who were trying to help him.

He couldn't imagine cheating on her. Fall out of love, fine. Talk about it, work it out, and decide to have an amicable split. But sleep around? With his boss, no less? Then, during the divorce, get half of everything he built on his wages while she stayed home and set up her trysts.

No fucking way.

Bashing her in the head felt good, but it also made him feel a little sad. After all they'd done together, how did it end up like this? He would've never dreamed of it. Had he the ability to see the future like Sarah, he wouldn't have married Kymberly.

Fireman style, he carried her outside, grabbed the ladder, and set everything down by the hole's edge.

Once Kym was in place, having Sarah exit with the balaclava was brilliant. He'd faked falling, made her think Kym was him lying there and stood back to video Sarah while she pummeled his ex-wife.

Once Sarah realized her mistake and removed the balaclava, she identified herself on the video for all to see.

A video will be anonymously sent to his contact, Blair Mackey, at the newspaper and anonymously uploaded to several social media sites.

By noon tomorrow, the search for Sarah Roberts would intensify. And Joel Blacken would come out on top as he would be the man to discover Sarah's body right alongside Kymberly Blacken's.

He followed Sarah inside and closed the door.

"What now?" Sarah asked, tilting to one side as she kept

the weight off her bad foot.

Blacken grabbed the duct tape off the counter and held it up. "I don't trust you. At all. So I have to tie you up."

"Not these ankles." She looked down. "Just try it. The pain would be too much."

"Fine. I'll roll some around your knees."

"What's the point?" she asked. "All this for what? I'm assuming you have a plan."

He nodded. "The plan is for you to be bound so I don't have to worry about you killing me."

"Bound or not, you should still worry."

He cracked a smile. "Charming. Now"—he gestured with his weapon—"on your knees, hands on the back of your head."

Sarah waited a moment. He stared at her, about to raise the weapon threateningly, when she lowered herself, using the counter for support. Once down, she clasped her hands behind her head.

He got behind her and undid a long strip of tape, then wound it over her wrists and allowed her to lower her arms past her chest.

"I'm leaving them bound at the front. Consider yourself lucky."

"This is lucky?"

Knowing Sarah's reputation for violence, he thought it a little strange she would allow him to control her so easily.

After her wrists were complete, Sarah laid on her side, and Blacken wrapped duct tape around her legs just below the knees, mindful to avoid her swollen ankle.

For some reason, working on Sarah made him feel like

he was trying to secure an active wasp nest to a fence. Be gentle, or the consequence is death.

"Tell me, Sarah, who knows you're here?"

"Here? No one knows where I am. Shit, I didn't even know I would be here until I got here."

He walked around to face her. She looked up at him sideways.

"Bullshit."

"Yeah? Okay, well, fuck you, too."

"Nice."

"You expected something else? Not too friendly of you to tie up guests."

"Uninvited guests. In other countries, I could've killed you on my property. Remember, consider yourself lucky."

"Got it." She nodded, looked down at her wrists, then back to Blacken. "Lucky. I see your point."

"Sarcasm must work for you."

She shrugged. "It has its moments."

He imagined the trouble it would take for her to untie herself and run from the cabin. A near impossibility with her ankle.

After several more moments of watching Sarah on the cabin's kitchen floor, he retrieved his ex-wife outside. Once Kymberly was on the living room floor, bound and gagged, he dragged Sarah over beside her and marveled at his masterpiece. This was his aim from day one. The Russell issue he hadn't expected. Jensen kidnapping him had been a nuisance. But now he had what he wanted. He could finish his plan and reenter society as a free man. No wife, no Sarah, and soon to be, no Jensen.

Back in the kitchen, he poured himself a drink.

He would relax. Possibly even sleep a little. It was almost over. Before sunrise, he would place both women in their final resting place and act out the final scene.

With a toast to good fortune, holding his beverage high in the empty kitchen, he then drank the whiskey in one go, poured another, and smiled at his genius.

He had won.

Chapter 41

It had been at least three hours since her wrists had been taped. Three hours of tossing and turning, searching for a comfortable position but finding none.

No mention of bathroom breaks, no food or drink. She heard Blacken drinking a couple of shots and then rummaging around somewhere.

He checked on them several times, but they had disappeared for the past half an hour. Had he fallen asleep?

Kymberly lay beside her, blood smearing her pretty face. After what Blacken had done to her—as described by Vivian, who had just made a mental appearance—Sarah felt even worse for having attacked her. Kymberly didn't deserve this. Whatever she had done to piss off her husband, this wasn't going to happen anymore. Abusive men, cop or not, had to pay for what they did. When Parkman and Aaron showed up, this entire ordeal would end.

She wanted to know how she came to be involved with any of it. Why her specifically, if it was just a marital issue, a disgruntled husband?

And why kill all those people on that prison bus?

After all she had done to learn to trust cops, could the ultimate betrayal come from the police themselves? If so, she would struggle to trust them forever after. Due to the actions of the few, she would paint them all with one brush, as she had in the past, and never trust them again. Life would get challenging because many members of law enforcement had come to her aid in the past.

She stared up at the wooden ceiling and wondered what to do, where to go, and what her sister was doing to set her free. She'd literally walked right into a trap upon Vivian's directions.

Aaron and Parkman were probably outside, watching the cabin. It had to be at least three or four in the morning. She hoped they would have devised some sort of plan to extricate her. Both men had been at this sort of thing long enough. With Parkman's history as a cop and Aaron's history as a wicked fighter, they could easily overpower one man, even if he was armed. They'd certainly done it before.

At least, she hoped so. She didn't like the alternative. Blacken had something planned for the morning, and Sarah was sure it involved her being unconscious underwater.

The evening, the morning, however she looked at it, seemed grim.

She started when something bumped beside the cabin.

Besides a soft light in the kitchen, the cabin's interior was dark. She pivoted around, new acid in her stomach at the prospect of what was coming, and waited for another sound.

Kymberly breathed quietly beside her, long and slow inhalation, elongated exhalation. Sarah waited, alert, awake.

Then it came again. Steps bounded away from the cabin.

Someone had been at the window, staring in. Chills formed goosebumps on her arms.

Parkman? Aaron?

Relief flooded through her. They were there. They had followed the directions properly. This would all be over in minutes.

They had watched and waited until Blacken passed out. It was perfect. She hadn't thought of it. The warning to stay away if there was a visible weapon was frivolous. Just wait until Blacken fell asleep, then access the cabin. It was only a summer cottage, for hell's sake. Easy access compared to homes in the city that could be alarmed to the hilt, cops minutes away.

She waited. Minutes passed, then more.

What were they waiting for? Blacken could wake for any reason.

Come now.

As if in response to her mental plea, something clicked outside near the front door. Interesting choice. Why the front door? A window, perhaps? The back door?

Someone fiddled with the lock, the sound deafening in the cabin.

Stop, guys! You're too loud.

She glanced at Kymberly—still out. She looked around,

but there was no sign of Blacken in the corridor to her right, in the kitchen.

She turned back to the front door as the metallic sound stopped.

Someone rattled the knob. From where she lay, it was easy to hear the protest of the still-locked door, but she couldn't see if the knob turned.

A moment later, they started in with the metallic sounds again.

The floor creaked to her right.

Blacken stood in the corridor, the gun held in both hands, out in front of him and aimed at the front door.

Her stomach dropped. Should she yell to warn them? What if it was a decoy? Draw Blacken to the front while one of them is at the back, waiting to enter? If so, brilliant, but still, Blacken might shoot through the door.

He edged closer to the front. Like before, the metallic clicking ceased. Then whoever stood on the other side of the door—Parkman or Aaron—gripped the knob and turned it.

Locked.

Blacken advanced another step. He was only a few steps from the wooden door now, steady on his feet.

She breathed in quiet gasps, pants, her stomach in knots. This wasn't supposed to be how her rescue played out. Blacken could fire through the wood. Whoever was trying to pick the lock wouldn't see his attacker. They would just feel the punch of the bullet.

Sarah opened her mouth to scream a warning when Blacken lowered the gun. She chose to stay silent, her head woozy from all the quiet panting.

The metallic sound returned as the person attempted to pick the lock one more time.

Blacken looked back at Sarah and raised a finger to his lips for quiet. Maybe he would let the lock-picker play out his game, then leave. Staying quiet meant he didn't want them to know anyone was home. Sarah could do that. She could wait.

Blacken stared at the door. Sarah stared at Blacken.

He stepped closer.

She frowned. What was he doing?

He stepped to within four feet of the door.

The metallic clicking stopped once more. They were going to try the knob. If the door opened, Blacken would have nowhere to hide. He was in the center of the living room, completely exposed.

The knob twisted. It kept twisting.

The door moved inward slightly.

They had done it. The lock was picked. The door to the cabin continued to open.

But Blacken didn't move. Her frown deepened. Confused, she opened her mouth to shout a warning.

The door opened more than a foot, the silhouette in the door the same shape and size as Aaron.

Blacken raised his weapon and fired at the same moment Sarah screamed.

Blacken fired again and again as the figure in the doorway jerked with each impact.

Tiny liquid spurts shot out of the silhouette, pantomiming a marionette doll with broken strings. The figure lost its footing, stepped back to regain his balance, and then dropped unmoving to the grass outside the door.

The cabin door closed on its own.

Sarah kept screaming. Not as a warning anymore. She was just screaming, yelling Aaron's name. Over and over.

Aaron was gone, and it was her fault.

Sarah wailed.

Chapter 42

Blacken lowered the empty gun, shut the door, and looked back at Sarah as she shouted. He should've gagged her when he tied her up, but he hadn't expected an intruder.

"Rescue attempt failed, eh Sarah?" he tried to shout over her agonized shrieks.

He'd hit the intruder, that was for sure. At least half of the bullets made contact. He'd even heard the thump as the man staggered backward under the fusillade and dropped to the ground.

His ex-wife was still out, and Sarah was slowly quieting into gurgling sobs. The pain she must feel, knowing whoever she asked to rescue her was dead.

Blacken's training kicked in. Years on the force had honed him to act like a machine in moments of high stress.

He strode to the side cabinet for a box of ammo. After reloading, he snatched the flashlight off the top of the cabinet and started back for the door.

One look at Sarah was all it took to see she was in a bad way. Curled up as close to a ball as she could, her forearms covered her face. The little of her cheek he saw was red and covered in tears. She vibrated with sobs.

He felt no pity, no sadness, nothing. She would be dead within hours, her pain gone with everything else.

At the door, he hesitated. He hadn't heard anyone else, though. To be safe, he placed his back against the wall beside the door, grabbed the knob with his left hand, the gun in his right, and eased the door open.

The front steps, the porch, and the grass beyond were empty.

The intruder was gone.

"Fuck," he muttered to himself.

He was sure he hit the guy. Several times, in fact. There was no way someone could survive that.

Unless they were dragged away.

That meant there were two out there.

Should he wait inside for them to reveal themselves? Or go outside, find them, and kill them?

Blacken refused to be a prisoner in his own home. He jumped through the open door and lowered himself against the wall to be less of a target.

He scanned the area for movement, listening to the night. Even though he'd done this sort of thing for years, he still got pumped up, his heart racing, his senses tuned into his surroundings.

The sky slightly lightened in the east. In an hour or so, the sun would rise. That gave him an hour to locate the intruder and finish the job.

He moved along the porch to the end. A quick glance around the corner showed the side of the cabin was empty. He did the same for the other end of the porch and saw nothing.

Whoever tried to break in was either behind the cabin or gone. They could have made the cover of trees. That would make sense.

Actually, nothing made sense. After being shot multiple times, how the hell was the intruder even alive?

He checked out the front of the cabin one more time, staring at the road to make sure he hadn't missed anyone watching him. It was dark, but his eyes had adjusted enough to see definition, and he didn't see a soul.

With the flashlight, he examined the front door and surrounding area. There was blood, but it was minimal. So, he didn't hit an artery, but he had hit the intruder.

Could he have missed more than he hit? The amount of blood led him to believe he had only grazed the intruder.

Could that be possible?

If so, that made sense that the man would be up and gone. A wounded perp taking multiple hits, enough to drop them, didn't run away.

Reshaping his theory, he leaned against the deck support near the front steps and stared across his property.

He had to check the back. There was no other way. There wasn't enough blood to follow a trail. The grass hadn't been cut in a month. It was high enough to cover spilled blood.

He killed the flashlight and stepped off the porch.

Night noises had quieted, a sense of danger in the air. He felt it more than he heard it. With each step, the grass soft, the ground moist with dew, he approached the rear of the cabin in absolute silence. Unless the perp saw him coming, he would not know how close Blacken was getting.

There had been no return fire. If the intruder carried a weapon, even out of reflex, it should've gone off. He assumed and hoped the intruder did not have a weapon.

At the back of the cabin, he dropped to his haunches and peered around the edge slowly. Nothing moved. Even with his eyes studying the landscape, surveying the ground for a bump, watching the line of trees for movement, he saw nothing.

The perp had to have gone somewhere. People didn't just disappear.

He rose to a standing position, listening.

A creak inside the cabin. Sarah turning over. Maybe Kym woke up. It didn't matter. They weren't going anywhere until he was ready to move them.

He waited, releasing his breath soundlessly, then inhaling. Wherever they were hiding, they would reveal themselves soon.

More creaking inside the cabin.

What the hell was Sarah doing?

He needed to check but didn't want to leave his post at the back of the cabin. The wounded intruder wouldn't be able to travel far. He had to be back here somewhere.

A footstep on the other side of the wall.

He turned to look at the cabin.

Was Sarah on her feet? If so, how? Her ankle was still swollen. Kym's ankles were secure.

Unless Sarah undid them.

He couldn't wait anymore. He had to check on his captives.

With one last look at the empty backyard of the cabin, he moved along the wall and glanced at the porch. Nothing had changed. The front door still sat ajar.

He strode to the steps, took both in one jump, and then shoved the door open all the way.

A man was bent over Sarah, undoing her wrists, her legs already freed.

She gasped and whispered something to the man.

Blacken raised his weapon and shot the man in the back before he had a chance to turn around.

Chapter 43

From the corner of her eye, Sarah watched as Blacken exited the cabin. She breathed through her mouth, her nose clogged with mucus from crying.

Aaron. Gone.

How was it possible? Why hadn't Vivian done something?

She was finished. It was over. There would be no more psychic shit, no more helping people. The cost was too high.

Her sister had allowed it to happen.

Fuck you, Vivian.

She rolled over and stared at the roof of the cabin, wondering when Blacken would kill her. Would she fight when the time came? Did she even care anymore?

She thought she heard Blacken step off the front porch,

then nothing. The waiting for the sound of a final bullet, ending the man she loved so dearly, grew maddening. How many times had she been tied up and at the whim of her captor? Would it ever end? What was the purpose? Why couldn't she do Vivian's bidding with less risk?

But it was too late for all that now. Aaron had been shot. He was likely dying somewhere out there, trying to stay hidden while Parkman worked something out.

The floor creaked by the door.

A man stood in the doorway, a large knife in his hand. She reared back and tried to sit up. Not sure if he was friend or foe, she remained quiet.

The man tread lightly, almost floating across the cabin floor toward her, the knife extended out front.

With a finger to his lips, he stopped in front of her, then kneeled by her legs and applied the knife to the tape that bound her.

As he sliced it apart, he leaned in close.

"My name is Russell. I tried to warn Parkman." He glanced at the door, then back to Sarah. "You should have stayed away from Blacken. He'll kill you, Sarah."

She nodded frantically, her heart skipping. "That was you? At the door?"

He nodded as the duct tape on her legs separated. Then he applied the knife to the tape on her wrists.

"He shot you," she said.

He tapped his chest. "Kevlar. Haven't taken it off in a week. He grazed my neck, but that was it." He checked the door, momentarily lost his balance, took a step to not fall over, and then addressed her. "Blacken is evil. Run from this place. Get as far away as you can."

Aaron wasn't dead. Blacken had shot the man in front of her. Aaron and Parkman were told to avoid the sight or sound of weapons. They were okay. Everything was okay. The man's words faded as she tried to focus on him. She nodded, barely registering the words.

Her wrists parted as the tape ripped.

Someone was at the front door. She peered around the man to see.

Blacken was in the cabin. His gun was up.

She whispered, "Behind you."

Blacken fired.

The man jerked forward with the impact of a bullet, sprawling out on the floor beside Kymberly.

He rolled to the side as another bullet tore up the floor an inch from his head. Then he launched his feet over his head, performed a back roll into the bedroom, and disappeared.

"Russell," Blacken shouted angrily, running for the bedroom door. "Why are you here?"

Sarah tried to stand, but her bad ankle couldn't handle even an ounce of weight, and she dropped to the floor, wincing at the pain.

Blacken flicked on the lights and stepped into the bedroom.

A knife swung down in the doorway from chest height, a shaft of light reflected off its clean surface the moment before it entered Blacken's forearm.

Russell was armed and fighting back.

Blacken shrieked and launched backward, his gun coming up in defense. He fired, but the bullet went wild as

Russell pushed the knife downward, knocking Blacken off balance.

The fight moved back into the living room. Through whatever pain Russell was dealing with after being shot at such close range—bruised or broken ribs—he'd lost his grip.

Now several feet apart, Blacken raised his weapon higher, where Kevlar wouldn't protect Russell.

"You fucking prick. Die—" Blacken fired.

The gun clicked empty or misfired.

He tried again. Nothing.

Russell didn't wait for confirmation the gun was empty. He rushed Blacken, diving on him from several feet away.

Sarah made it to her one good foot and hopped in place momentarily, watching the men roll on the ground, arms flailing.

Blood trailed from Blacken's arm. Russell wailed in pain but didn't lose any ground. Pent-up anger drove Russell in his attack. Sarah had seen it before. Some fight to stay alive. Some fight because they're supposed to. But then there were the fighters who had an emotional attachment to the win. A man fighting another because he was cut off in traffic is a whole different battle than a man fighting the rapist of his teen daughter.

Russell, if given the chance, would kill Blacken with his bare hands. But Blacken held him back, bad arm and all.

Sarah had to help. Stunned into immobility, her ankle shooting barbs of pain into her skull, she'd watched, hoping Russell would knock Blacken out or worse.

She grabbed a thick book off the mantel to her left, hefted it, and then decided not to throw it. Instead, she grabbed a thick ashtray.

With one solid hop, then another, she stood over the men who looked like blood-covered wrestlers, panting and red-faced, at the end of their fight.

She raised the ashtray, moved a little to the left, and smashed it toward Blacken's face.

He moved with less than a second to spare, the ashtray connecting harmlessly with the wooden floor.

A foot shot out, knocking into the back of Sarah's knee, collapsing her good leg.

She fell beside the men, her bad ankle slamming on the floor, and shouted in pain.

The knife had been freed. Russell and Blacken were in a death grip, both holding the hilt between them.

Sarah rolled away, clenched her hand into a fist, and drove it into the side of Blacken's face. His head moved with the blow, then centered on Russell again, the fight between them unfinished.

The knife edged toward Russell.

Sarah drove her fist into Blacken again. Then again.

Blood seeped from Blacken's nose and his mouth, but the two hands pushing the knife closer to Russell did not let up.

Russell was losing his strength.

She decided to go for the man's balls. Blacken might be able to take shots to the face like a UFC fighter, but could he handle repeated shots to the balls?

She edged along the floor, wishing her ankle wasn't in such bad shape. Before she could set up, Russell melted to the floor, pushing her farther away.

She glanced up at the men. Blood pulsed from Russell's

neck where the knife had entered.

Blacken yanked it out and thrust it in again. Out and in.

Sarah screamed for him to stop, then launched on top of them, trying to pull Blacken off.

Something banged into her foot. The pain was so intense her vision blurred at the edges.

Russell's body fell to the side, Sarah with it.

Then Blacken was up, a feral expression on his blood-covered face. Pints of Russell's blood had sprayed all over Blacken, his upper body drenched in a grotesque display of the macabre.

Sarah fought for consciousness as the pain in her leg became overwhelming.

Russell gurgled blood, a little bubbling out the sides of his mouth. He'd taken bullets for her, risked his life to free her, and now he was dying on Blacken's floor as if it meant nothing.

Yet he was smiling.

In his eyes, she saw peace.

On his last breath, as Blacken stood over them, the bloody knife held firmly in his grasp, Russell mouthed *Thank you* to Blacken.

Blacken nodded at Russell like they were old warriors, one honoring the other's chance to die honorably.

Whatever it was between the two men, it was over.

Russell was gone.

"Up," Blacken ordered. "Now it's your turn."

Chapter 44

Within thirty minutes, Blacken had Sarah in the back of his car, her wrists bound again. He'd bound her legs as well, but the pain had decreased. Her ankle had grown numb.

Kymberly Blacken was still unconscious, tied up beside Sarah.

Vivian had shown up, whispering hints that it would work out. This was the way it was supposed to go. Somehow, she intimated, this was her plan all along.

She glanced up at Blacken, who was doing something outside the vehicle.

"So, what now?" She held up her bound hands. "Huh?"

Blacken's face was still stained. As much as he tried to get Russell's blood off, it remained in his pores. He'd wrapped his wounded arm, but blood seeped through that as well.

"Your video was already uploaded. People around the world are watching the fugitive Sarah Roberts attacking the wife of the detective investigating her." He hitched up his pants. "After I've dealt with you, I'm taking my wife to the hospital."

Blacken's eyes had taken on a manic look. When he stared at Sarah, something was missing.

"Russell was a friend. And he tried to kill me today."

"Blacken, you shot him. Of course, he would fight back."

"Russell owed me." Blacken stepped away, shaking his head. "It wasn't supposed to be like this. Everything's out of control now."

Blacken moved to the front of the vehicle, leaned down, and checked something under the grill. He moved to the side of the vehicle and then disappeared under it.

Sarah waited until he reappeared, the sun slowly rising on a new day. Her body shook from the lack of food and spent adrenaline. Watching Russell die on the cabin floor bothered her deeply. He had tried to do the right thing. Regardless of what he had done in his life, he was attempting to set the record straight.

Blacken had told her that Russell had orchestrated the attack on the prison bus. He was paying a debt owed to important people.

Russell hadn't known his brother would be on that bus, though, and had since lost his mind. She couldn't trust anything Blacken said, even if she wanted to. He kept saying it was over; no more killing, no more fighting. But Sarah couldn't live. She knew too much—like incriminating evidence against Blacken.

With Sarah gone, maybe then it could be over.

Blacken popped up again beside the car. He climbed into the driver's seat and headed down the road Sarah had walked in on.

She thought about reaching over the seat and fighting him. In other circumstances, she would. He was wounded and probably quite tired after fighting Russell.

But Vivian had said to wait. Where was Blacken taking them? The lake Vivian spoke of the other day? Wasn't she supposed to be unconscious in the lake? What more would happen before it was the end for her?

The years added up. The time spent fighting, being beaten, held captive, and having to kill. She'd lost friends along the way. She was tired. She needed a break.

A darkness that consumed her many years ago reared its ugly head. Depression brought on her hair-pulling episodes as a teenager. Since then, she had gained so much. Friends, laughter, experiences, and all her hair back, along with confidence and strength.

But she'd also lost a lot.

She'd lost her life. There was no white picket fence, no end in sight, no vacation, and no real romance. She and Aaron saw each other when they could. It seemed other people's lives mattered more.

A dark part of her felt like giving up, letting go. The warring part of her was determined to fight on, make things right, and do it on her terms.

She would rest her head back and close her eyes for the moment. She was tired, exhausted, and spent.

For the moment, she would listen to Vivian and see where Blacken was taking her. For the moment, she wouldn't give up. Not Sarah. She wasn't a quitter.

She was in her sister's trusting hands as she sat in the back seat of Blacken's car.

Chapter 45

BLACKEN CHECKED HIS MIRRORS. The two-lane highway was virtually empty this far north of Toronto at such an early hour.

He only had ten more minutes to drive before Sarah and his ex-wife would be out of his life for good. Plans didn't always work out, and he wasn't even sure this plan would work, but however they got to the end game, they were there now. This was where he wanted to be, minus Russell's body in the bathtub. He would have to deal with that.

Things got messed up, but when did they not? He could deal with it. Whatever was thrown at him, he'd deal.

A glance over his shoulder revealed both women were out. His ex-wife still hadn't regained consciousness, and it appeared Sarah might have fallen asleep. Awake all night and now lying down in the car's back seat, the subtle shaking of travel must have lulled her to sleep. He remained alert, though. Sarah was good. She could easily be faking it and jump over the seat at any moment.

The twisted ankle had subdued her enough to keep her manageable, which he was grateful for. If she hadn't twisted her ankle, he probably would've had to injure her enough to subdue her until this final play.

The lake came up on the right. He drove the speed limit, only passing two cars as he approached the spot he had already surveyed.

An early morning fisherman sat on a boat in the distance. Why the hell would anyone want to wake up at such an hour to go fishing? The same goes for golfing. He just didn't understand.

Blacken pulled over into the lookout section on the side of the highway and took in the spectacular view. The empty gravel parking area of the lookout could hold a dozen cars and was at least fifty feet above the lake below. A sharp drop at the cliff's edge was a popular spot for teenagers in the summer to film themselves jumping into the water and then posting it on YouTube.

Blacken lowered all the car windows. He needed the car to take on as much water as possible. He opened his door quietly and got out of the car. He retrieved a block of wood in the trunk and then left the lid slightly open.

After one last look around, he opened the back door and used a pocket knife to slice through Sarah's duct tape. Her wrists and legs were free, and he nudged her shoulder.

Drowsy, her eyelids fluttered until she woke.

She had actually fallen asleep. This wasn't the Sarah Roberts he'd heard of. She was a mad dogfighter to the bitter end.

"Wake up, Sarah." He shook her shoulder. "I need you to drive my wife to the hospital."

Sarah got up and rubbed her eyes. It took her a moment to realize she was untied. She slapped the side of her face twice, then started to get out of the car. He helped her to stand, then closed the back door and eased her into the driver's seat of the idling car.

"Which way?" she asked. "North or south?"

"North or south? You know your direction from here? How? You were sleeping."

She pointed toward the rising sun. "That's east." She pointed forward. "That's north." Then, she pointed over her shoulder, her eyes still half-lidded. "That's south. Which way?"

"South," he said, knowing she wouldn't be going anywhere but south, technically. "You ready, Sarah?"

She nodded and made to put the car in gear.

"Wait."

She stopped.

"There's one more thing."

She looked up at him, a hand on her forehead to cover the glare in her eyes.

"This." He held up the block of wood.

She studied it for a moment, a frown behind the hand on her forehead.

"What's this thing—"

Blacken rammed the block into Sarah's head. She

snapped sideways in the seat, moaning.

He dragged her back up to a sitting position, blood forming near her temple. Then he rammed her again.

Her arms flopped, and she dropped to the car seat. This time, she wasn't sleeping. This time, she was out cold. As unconscious as the ex-wife in the back seat.

After one more look at the highway, he put the car in gear, left the parking brake on, and leaned down to the gas pedal to set the chunk of wood on it. The engine revved and jumped forward a little, knocking him back.

As the car edged forward, the engine fighting the parking brake, Blacken reached inside, disengaged the parking brake, and jumped back, but he wasn't fast enough.

The doorframe knocked into his shoulder and spun him out of the vehicle. He landed on his butt in the dirt as his car hurtled toward the scenic outlook's edge.

The trunk popped open as the car left solid ground, doing at least forty kilometers per hour.

It was the last of his car he would ever see as it plummeted out of sight to the lake fifty feet below the edge of the cliff.

He got to his feet and stared out at the lake, staying back from the edge. The single boat in the distance held one occupant as far as he could tell. The man—gender at this distance was difficult, so he guessed—had turned at the sound of the car going in.

The man yanked his fishing line out of the water, turned on his outboard motor, and started toward the fallen car.

Blacken hid behind a tree near the edge. At the water, with Sarah's door and the trunk open, water rushed in, sinking the vehicle rather quickly. It was already half submerged.

The boat was too far away.

After several moments of watching his car sink to a watery grave, Blacken glanced at the boat. It hadn't even crossed half the distance.

Then the car was gone, water closing in over the back bumper.

The boat engine revved high but wasn't going fast enough to save anyone. The women had possibly a minute left. The boat would take four or five minutes more to even be in the area, let alone dive down and fetch bodies.

Blacken headed for the trees on the other side of the highway, hoping to make it before a random vehicle came around the bend. The only thing that could ruin him now were witnesses.

He made the tree line on the other side of the highway without incident.

One more look over his shoulder revealed the boater was still en route to the area where his car entered the lake.

It was over.

It was truly over.

Sarah Roberts was dead. Kymberly Blacken was dead, killed by the woman who had kidnapped her. At least, that was how the story would play out.

All the puzzle pieces were in place for Blacken to reclaim his life.

He walked through the woods a new man, knowing all he had left to do was deal with Russell's body back at the cabin.

A wide grin broke out on his face.

He'd done it. He'd won. He'd finally done it.

"Fuck you, Sarah," he muttered to himself. "I win."

Jensen was next.

Chapter 46

Something crashed into her chest. Pain erupted through her breasts and ribs. She moaned and pushed away from whatever was on her.

Water gushed everywhere. A large fountain, a hose must've broken. A deep cold enclosed her feet and crept up her shins. Her head ached, making it hard to open her eyes. She tried to orient herself but felt dizzy, like she had lost all balance. Was she in a boat? If so, how did she get there?

It grew dark quickly. Her eyelids fluttered, then opened, then closed.

Vivian shouted something in her consciousness.

Memories flooded back. Blacken. Aaron being shot. But it wasn't Aaron. Blacken killing Russell. Blacken's car. The wooden block.

The lake.

She snapped awake. Water engulfed Blacken's car as it sank. Blood flowed freely from her head.

Kymberly Blacken fought to get out, pressing herself between the two front seats. She was awake and looked just as dazed as Sarah felt.

The car was sinking fast. All the windows were down, water rushing in from everywhere. In the mirror, the open trunk obscured her view of where they had fallen from. The car tilted at a forty-five-degree angle, hood aiming for the deep. The engine's weight dragged them down, the remaining air trapped inside the car being forced out.

Upon impact, the airbags had punched her in the chest. Between panic and the airbag, she labored for each breath.

She snapped out of momentary confusion and struggled to get out, but the car door wouldn't budge. The water pressed in, cutting off any chance of exit.

Water covered her legs and rose above her waist. The water roared its way inside the car.

Sarah pushed herself upward, careful not to bump her bad ankle, then turned to Kymberly. She nodded at the open window. Blacken's wife had the same idea.

Sarah held a hand up for Kymberly to wait until the car equalized with water. Currently, the cascade entering the car was too great to push through it.

In Blacken's attempt to sink them fast by leaving the windows open, he had enabled their escape route. But how far would the car sink before they could swim out?

The morning sunlight faded as they dropped below the surface.

How deep could the lake be so close to a cliff?

The last bit of air was trapped near the roof and seeping toward the back window in the passenger corner. Sarah took several gulps of air, ducked her head in the water, and pushed out the window. Minus a small bump where the top of the window connected with her lower back, she was out easily.

She opened her eyes in the gloom and watched the eerie sight of the car sink lower into the black depths of the lake.

Not a free diver, she was aware her time underwater was limited. Possibly half a minute, maybe a full minute was her maximum.

But where was Blacken's wife? Why hadn't she followed Sarah out?

She floated face down, watching the tail lights sink lower without any sign of Kymberly.

She should have stayed. She should've held onto the car at the window frame and helped Kymberly out.

Her chest heaved, the air already becoming a request.

She dipped lower, kicking with her one good foot, thrusting with her arms to descend. The car was gone, swallowed by the murky water.

Sarah would be forced to surface if Kymberly didn't show up within seconds.

She looked upward. The dim image of a watery sky seemed far away. Doubt entered her thoughts. Could she even make the surface if she raced for it at that moment?

Vivian? We cool here?

She focused on calm as her chest rose and fell in a rhythmic ballet of attempting to obtain air. It had worked her entire life this way, so her lungs weren't sure why it wasn't working now.

One last glimpse below.

No Kymberly.

She mentally chastised herself. How could she just let her die? How selfish to swim out of the car without ensuring Kym was behind her.

She could have easily grabbed the window frame, held onto the car, then reached inside and helped Kymberly swim out.

They would have both lived.

Instead, Kymberly had dropped to her death, and Sarah would die from waiting too long for her.

After one last look below, her chest about to force her mouth open in search of air, Sarah kicked her good foot. The swollen one moved slightly, a wince forcing her mouth open. She kept her teeth tight together, her throat closed, as she reached above her head and pumped her arms for the surface.

She pumped, pushed, and swam, but the surface was too far away. Unable to determine how far she had swum, her chest aching for breath, she glanced upward one last time.

The surface shimmered with sunshine. The distant drone of an engine floated to her. Water cocooned her and enveloped her.

She thought about letting go, about joining Vivian.

She blinked. The surface had to be at least a couple of dozen feet away.

She wouldn't make it. Oxygen was depleted, her strength gone, her chest on fire.

Alone, she waited until her body took over her will to survive. She chose to keep her mouth closed. She was choosing not to breathe. But her body had other plans, and those plans would kill her.

She blinked once more. Whispered Vivian's name, Aaron's name. Thought about Parkman. Whispered a goodbye to them, saddened she wouldn't see Darwin and Rosina again.

One last look upward. The surface seemed farther away. She'd been sinking.

Then she opened her mouth, releasing the air she'd held.

Closed her mouth.

She closed her eyes.

Then opened her mouth to breathe.

Chapter 47

SOMETHING MOVED BESIDE HER.

A diver.

He shoved his hand toward her face. He held something attached to a cord. That something entered her open mouth, and her lips closed on it.

Her lungs expanded.

Sarah inhaled from the spare regulator attached to Aaron's oxygen tanks. Her thoughts cleared, her mind sharpened, and she pulled out the regulator—Vivian had called it an octopus in her note to Aaron and Parkman—then swam for the surface. Aaron held her back, his grip strong, fins on his feet.

All she wanted was to be on the surface, breathing normally again. Now that she had a reprieve, the water around her felt more like a coffin than a lake.

He pulled something up beside her, a long cylindrical device that hummed. The diver propulsion vehicle Vivian had told them to rent along with the boat and the scuba gear. Parkman would be in the boat, Aaron in the water.

He wrapped an arm around her waist, and with the propulsion vehicle held out in front, they started through the water on a slight angle toward the sun, the air.

The idea wasn't to break the surface within five minutes of going over. Just in case, Blacken stayed behind to watch his car sink. And when they did break the surface, it wouldn't be anywhere near where the car went in.

Her chest ached, but she was alive. She'd swallowed water and coughed a couple of times, but overall, they would make it.

The note about being unconscious when Aaron met up with her was slightly inaccurate. She *had* been unconscious but had awakened in the car several moments before Aaron's arrival.

Saddened by Kymberly's demise, she watched the surface edge closer, internally begging Aaron to rise faster.

Thrusting upward with his fins, he pushed her toward the air above. A moment later, she broke the surface and gasped the rich scent of sweet air until she felt lightheaded.

Aaron held her close, making it easy for her to breathe and collect herself without having the effort of swimming. He waited, and she was grateful for the moment to clear her head.

Water broke behind them.

Sarah jolted in his arms and spun around, water sloshing

over her shoulders.

Another diver held Kymberly.

"What …?" Sarah managed to say.

Aaron popped out his regulator. "Meet Bethany Carpenter. My scuba instructor."

Sarah stared at the other diver as Bethany ensured Kymberly was breathing fine. Kymberly laid her head back in the water and stared skyward as the instructor held her.

She turned to Sarah, and their eyes met. "Aaron was an easy student. Disciplined and fit. He took to the water like a natural."

Sarah glanced at Aaron, back at Bethany, and then at Aaron again. "You brought someone with you?" She glanced over his shoulder to see Parkman approaching in a small boat.

Aaron nodded. "I'm too new to this diving thing. Didn't want to do it alone. Looks like having the second diver saved another life."

"I couldn't find her," Sarah said. "Once I was clear of the car …" she swallowed, "and saw the taillights disappear, I thought she was gone with the car."

Bethany shook her head. "We had a bead on the car the whole time. I told Aaron to grab you. I followed the car down and got her out." Bethany smiled at everyone. "Good deed of the day, eh?"

Sarah held onto Aaron, tightening her grip around his neck. "Can we trust her?"

Aaron nodded. "Implicitly."

"You can trust me, Sarah. I took a student diving today. We both went home. End of story."

Sarah had her breathing back under control. A dull ache resonated in her head, and her foot felt better in the cold water. What bothered her was how many people were involved in knowing she was alive.

The world needed to think she was dead, according to Vivian.

Parkman and Aaron were no issue. But now they had Kymberly Blacken, the wife of the man who tried to kill her, and a dive instructor named Bethany Carpenter.

"Fair enough," Sarah said. "If Aaron vouches for you, we're good."

"Sarah, I've loved you from afar for years. From what I hear, you need a vacation. A long one. My lips are sealed."

"Thank you."

Parkman pulled up alongside them. "We gettin' out of here?" A toothpick stuck out of the side of his mouth.

"Please. I've had enough—"

Vivian cut her off. An idea was planted in her mind. It felt like someone else had added a file to her computer. At first, it was unfamiliar, something she wasn't sure about. But once she opened the thought—akin to opening the file—she saw the wisdom of the idea.

Vivian, it's brilliant.

"Sarah?" Aaron said. "You okay?"

She turned to him. "Yeah. We're good. Sorry, Vivian said something."

Parkman leaned down and extended a hand by the ladder at the back of the boat.

"Something to deal with right away?" he asked.

Sarah took his hand and climbed up onto the boat, careful

to only apply weight to her good foot.

"Something to deal with in a couple of hours."

Aaron climbed up behind her and turned to help Kymberly and Bethany. Parkman started back toward the captain's chair.

Once on board, Kymberly looked around at everyone.

"Who are you people?" she asked.

Chapter 48

BLACKEN FOUND DISPOSING OF Russell's body relatively easy despite his injured arm. The cabin was so secluded that he simply dragged Russell outside and dropped him in the pit. He could fill the pit high enough to cover the body with the spade. After sprinkling cayenne pepper and black pepper on the body to ward off wild animals in search of a meal, he worked into the late afternoon with the spade.

The final act was the camouflage cover. Once in place with leaves and twigs thrown over it for effect, Blacken only had to clean up the blood inside the cabin.

An hour into scrubbing, he decided to finish later. Sarah and his ex-wife were dead. Russell was dead. No one else was coming, which left him all the time in the world to scrub the evidence away.

To be truly successful and win, he needed to deal with Jensen. He was a decorated detective. His word would hold weight. But Blacken had been tied up in Jensen's basement. Travis Jensen had some explaining to do.

He grabbed his burner phone, dialed Blair Mackey at the newspaper, and filled him in on the stolen car. He'd finally caught up with Sarah. She had his wife, but he lost them near Huntsville. He would report his vehicle as stolen soon, but he got Blair to run with the story.

When he finished with Blair, he made an anonymous call to the Ontario Provincial Police detachment in Huntsville to tell them he thought he saw a car go into the lake from the lookout. He described his own car as a brown four-door sedan. He'd said that was all he could remember, then got off the phone.

One more call to report his car stolen and who he suspected was the thief, and then he was finished.

Minutes after his last call, Blacken removed the battery from the burner phone and stomped on both pieces. The phone was destroyed. He tossed it in the trash and headed outside into the late afternoon sun.

He began to walk, a free man. No wife, no ties to Russell, and nothing holding him back. Making sure Sarah was involved from the beginning, besmirching her name, was a flimsy plan at best. But if she were really psychic, she would come looking for him sooner rather than later in an effort to clear her name.

And what better person to kill prisoners? She was a vigilante, after all. And didn't vigilantes hunt bad guys? Those men on that bus were *convicted* bad guys. Of course, that made sense.

So, he blames that on Sarah and takes his cheating wife to the cabin where he holds her prisoner, announcing to the world—through Blair Mackey—that Kymberly is missing and Sarah Roberts is involved in some way.

Sarah would come. He was sure of it. Worst case, he had her number. He could just call her. But as it happened, he didn't have to. Sarah came, as he suspected she would.

And now it was all over. Sarah and his ex-wife would be found in his stolen car at the bottom of the lake.

Sarah would be remembered as a murderer who never stood trial for the murder of thirteen men on that bus and Kymberly Blacken.

Blacken kept walking. The sun was setting and would be down before he reached the highway.

He would get to Huntsville, rent a car, and drive to Toronto, where he would make a statement about Jensen's affair with his wife and how when he went to Jensen's house, he was tied up and forced to piss into a grate.

There was a skip in his step. It was all coming together. There was nothing left to deal with but tiny details. Jensen would pay—with his life if Blacken could arrange it—but Jensen would pay.

He reached the highway a half hour later, the sun almost gone, put out his thumb, and walked backward. A car would come. He could reassure them he was a safe ride by showing them his ID.

"My car was stolen," he would say. "Can you believe it?"

After several cars passed, he faced forward and kept walking.

His phone vibrated in his back pocket. A text had come through. He fished his phone out of his pocket and glanced at the screen.

It was a picture of Sarah and Kymberly. Their hair was wet like they'd been in a lake. They were smiling.

"This isn't possible," he muttered to himself, a pit forming in his stomach. He stopped walking. "Not possible."

A text followed, the phone vibrating in his hand.

Meet us at the art studio on Richmond Street in Toronto. It's the only one a block east of Spadina. Tomorrow morning at nine.

We have a deal for you. It'll keep you out of prison.
Come alone.

Blacken tightened his grip on the phone and started running, the bandage on his arm soaked through with blood.

Chapter 49

THEY SETTLED IN THE hotel after spending the day returning the rented boat, dropping off Bethany Carpenter and her scuba gear, and filling Kymberly in on what her husband had been up to.

After dinner, having kept a low profile and ensuring they didn't break any traffic laws, Sarah had them drive to Lacee Faust's motel in Toronto for the night. One more night in Toronto without the threat of someone calling the police was all they needed.

Once Janet Kirsten had checked them in—beyond happy Sarah had returned—she gave them a room that faced the back. No charge.

Several of the rooms were still sectioned off with yellow police tape as investigators continued to collect evidence of the murders that took place. But the motel was open for business, although it was a bit slow.

The four of them got in the room with a promise that Lacee's café was preparing dinner for them.

Sarah called Casper and brought him up to date.

"Wow, Sarah," Casper said after listening to everything. "You've been through a lot."

"I still need your help."

"I'm listening."

"Parkman and Aaron did nothing wrong. They've only been involved in helping me. The OPP tried to arrest them at a roadside restaurant—"

"I know all about it. A BOLO was issued for both of them."

"Can you get it canceled?"

"Not likely."

"What should they do?"

"Turn themselves in. Straighten it out."

"Smart play—under normal circumstances. But the cops think Aaron and I were involved in the prison bus attack."

"What about you? A Canada-wide manhunt is underway for you."

"I'm covered. Don't worry about me."

"Sarah." Casper's tone was cautionary. "What are you planning? Please don't tell me you're going to run."

"Okay, I won't."

"You're not running, are you?"

"No."

"Then what?"

"Casper, a man named Rob Russell, was responsible for

the attack on the bus. Aaron and I just tried to stop it."

"Russell. I know that name. He's the missing cop."

"You'll likely find his body at Blacken's cabin. Joel Blacken killed him last night."

"You were saying. But Blacken doesn't have a cabin in northern Ontario in his name."

"Search harder. You'll find it. North of Huntsville, out toward Clear Lake."

"I'll find it."

"Look in the pit out back. Something tells me you'll find what you're looking for there."

"Something or someone?"

"Just keep looking. You'll find everything you need in Blacken's cabin. DNA evidence will be everywhere to corroborate my story."

"As much as I believe you, I'll need evidence to get this shit off your head for sure."

"And you'll find it. Also, Russell's pickup truck is a mile from the cabin. Search it, too."

"Done. What about you and those men of yours?"

"Until we're cleared, I've got us covered."

"Covered how?"

"Casper?"

"Yeah?"

"Covered."

"Got it. Thanks, Sarah."

"Talk soon, my friend."

"Will do."

"And remember, I'll always be watching over you."

Casper cleared his throat. A moment later, not a fan of

goodbyes, the phone clicked. He'd hung up.

Sarah set down the phone.

"Now it's time to text Travis Jensen."

"You have his number?" Kymberly asked.

"My sister gave it to me," Sarah said, reaching for a burner phone Parkman had picked up.

"Your sister? The one who is dead?"

"Yeah."

Kymberly glanced at Aaron. Aaron shrugged. She looked at Parkman, who also shrugged.

Sarah watched her confusion form into a frown, searching the room for an answer.

"Don't worry, Kym," Sarah said. "My sister's cool. I know her better dead than I ever knew her when she was alive."

Kymberly had a faraway stare in her eyes, a dazed look of bewilderment. "Right." She nodded. "Okay."

Sarah typed the text to Jensen, then hit send.

Someone knocked on the door. A familiar voice whispered through it, "Dinner's ready."

"Lacee." Sarah got up and opened the door, her bad foot already able to handle small amounts of weight. "So good to see you. Come on in."

Once the door was closed, they invited Lacee to eat with them. Ten minutes into the meal of pasta and grilled lamb steaks with steamed spinach, another knock on the door interrupted them.

Janet had brought a complimentary bottle of wine.

Sarah took in the room and the people around her and wondered how different her life would be without her gift, her ability to hear her sister.

She watched as they all laughed, listened to their stories, and understood what love was and how she felt about Parkman and Aaron.

Tomorrow, all that would change. She wouldn't be checking into motels ever again.

Tomorrow would be the official last day on Earth for her. Everyone in the room and all the witnesses Vivian had planned to be there would confirm it.

Tomorrow, Sarah Roberts was scheduled to die. Then, no one could mess with her again.

No one could ever betray her again, either.

Tomorrow ended it all.

Chapter 50

They woke early. Lacee had left after dinner the previous evening, taking the dishes with her.

Sarah had pulled Lacee aside at the last minute and asked a huge favor. Lacee listened to everything and agreed without hesitation. She would bring her passport and have the minivan at the dog park just after the lunch hour, stocked with food and gas. Then she was gone. Parkman wouldn't let her go without paying something, so she agreed to take a tip. He forced a twenty into her pocket. She hugged everyone and left happier—and fuller—than when she had arrived.

The four of them got ready quickly. By seven in the morning, they were on the Gardiner Expressway heading toward the Spadina Avenue exit.

Sarah patted her pants pocket where the key to the art

studio sat. It was still there after all she had been through. She wondered if Adam DePont, the painter with the broken finger, had even noticed in his trauma and hospital visit that it was gone yet. If he had seen it missing and returned to change the locks, the entire plan would rely on breaking into the studio. Either way, Sarah needed access to the first-floor unit for everything to work.

This was her final play. Orchestrated and endorsed by Vivian.

Her attempt at helping random strangers to bolster her name with the public as the police continued their manhunt for her had a double meaning, and Vivian knew it all along.

Reaching out to Jessica was pointless. Her brother, Rob Russell, was killed anyway. Stopping the robbery guy, Winters, and his friend Ernesto and getting Percy to leave his cheating wife would bear fruit soon. Even breaking DePont's finger and stealing his art studio key would benefit Sarah. Far more than the simple random act of helping others.

All those people would be witnesses to her death and tell the world.

Only Vivian could've known that. When Sarah questioned her, Vivian explained that everyone everywhere had issues, something Sarah could help with. An abusive partner, a cheating lover, a criminal in the family, a future mugging, a rape. Everyone had a future with shit coming their way.

Vivian made sure to help the people who needed it most and those who enabled an end-game scenario for Sarah to get out from under her current issue.

Helping those people randomly on the streets of Toronto

would pay dividends in getting Blacken and Jensen off her back.

By killing me? Sarah had asked. *That kind of removes all issues, doesn't it?*

Vivian hadn't responded. She never responded well to sarcasm.

Parkman parked a few blocks up Spadina to the left of Richmond Street in a city lot. Once out of the car and near the studio, they stopped beside bushes at the front access to the building.

Sarah pointed along the brick wall. "See those double doors?"

Aaron nodded. "They look like barn doors."

"Those are the ones you leave by, Parkman." She looked at Kymberly. "You too. When this is over, you must leave with Parkman. He'll keep you safe." She turned her attention back to Parkman. "When this ends, get her to her husband's office. She'll need to make a complete statement, along with yourself, as to what had transpired over the last few days." Moving her gaze from Kymberly to Parkman, she stopped on Kymberly's face again. "Tell them everything. It's the only way to release you from any responsibility."

Kymberly nodded. "I wish this was already over."

"Me too." Sarah checked her watch. "It's almost eight. Jensen and Blacken should be here soon." She glanced up and scanned the people around them. "Unless they came early. Jensen's the one I'm most worried about. His connection to Lombardi bothers me."

Sarah surveyed the morning business people, the taxis, the cars rushing to make the yellow light, the honking impatience, the smell of morning, the thirst for coffee. She steeled herself for what she had to do and turned back to her friends.

"We ready?" she asked.

They nodded in turn, Kymberly looking the most nervous.

Sarah touched her arm. "You'll do fine. Remember, your husband tried to kill you and make it look like I did it. Jensen set you up. You're no stupid woman. You just got caught between two ambitious men. Their god is money, not love."

She nodded and leaned into Sarah for a hug. "What should I say?" Kymberly asked.

"Say nothing or say what comes naturally to you. Just be here until Parkman takes you out those doors."

"Why am I leaving early?"

Sarah eased her back to look into Kymberly's eyes. "You don't want to be here after nine in the morning. Trust me."

"What's going to happen?"

Sarah snuck a glance at Aaron. "Let's just say the end of the meeting will be explosive."

Kymberly nodded and wiped her eyes. "I'm so done with both those men."

"We all are."

Parkman started up the stairs. "We should go. Get off the street."

Sarah nodded, then handed the key to Aaron. "Unlock the studio. Get situated. I'll be there within ten minutes."

He frowned. "What are you going to do?"

"Think of it as a little reconnoitering. I have a few people to talk to before I go inside."

"Sarah—"

"Trust me, Aaron. It's the only way." She closed his fingers over the art studio key. "Go. It's okay."

"If she says it's okay, I'd go with it," Parkman said.

Aaron started up the steps, leading Kymberly toward the door. Once the three of them entered the building, Sarah started back toward Spadina. At the lights, she turned right and crossed Richmond.

A few doors up, she entered a busy coffee shop, cut across the floor, meandering through the sea of tables, and sat at an occupied table.

Adam DePont looked up and reared back.

"What the fuck do you want? Here to break another finger?"

"I need your help this morning."

"Fuck you. I ain't helping you with shit. You ruined my hand. I can't paint for over a month now."

Sarah gestured for him to stay seated, rose from her chair, and moved two tables over. She touched a woman's arm.

Jessica Russell turned to look at her. "What the …?"

"Please, come sit with us." She gestured at Adam. "We should talk."

"I tried to call my brother this morning. After thinking about what you said," she shrugged, "I guess it wouldn't hurt to warn him."

"Thank you for that, but I need a little something from you today. Please." She gestured at Adam's table. The artist looked absolutely horrified. The woman who broke his finger had invited a stranger to his table. He was probably wondering what would happen to him, but like a rubbernecker, he couldn't look away.

Once seated at Adam's table, Sarah said, "We wait. Two more people are joining us."

"For what?" Adam said. "I should leave. After what you did to me—in fact, I should call the police." His voice rose on the last word.

Sarah glared at him. "Keep your voice down."

His lips tightened, but he stayed silent.

"What's he talking about?" Jessica asked.

"Adam is an artist with a temper. He hurt a woman. Because of that, I hurt him." Sarah pointed at the broken finger.

Adam's red face lost color when another woman saw him for who he was.

"But it's okay, Adam," Sarah soothed. "Today, we make it all right."

He held up his bandaged finger. "This didn't make it right?"

Sarah shook her head. "Not yet."

Someone stopped beside their table. Sarah looked up into Percy's eyes.

"Oh, hey. You again."

Sarah stood. "You left her?"

Percy nodded. "Thank you. I did. And I feel so much better."

"Good. Please join us. We should talk."

Percy frowned as he looked down at Jessica and Adam. Then he shot a hand out to shake. Introductions were completed, and the four of them sat at the table, Adam being the only one with coffee in front of him. They all explained what Sarah had done to them individually two days ago.

Sarah checked her watch.

"We can't wait for the fourth to show." She shrugged. "Maybe he won't."

"What's this all about?" Adam asked.

Sarah looked from Jessica to Adam to Percy, then back to Jessica.

"You all know who I am?"

They nodded.

"And that the authorities are looking for me?"

They nodded again.

"And yet, none of you called them on me."

Adam grunted. "I almost did." He looked at his finger, then back to Sarah. "But deep down inside, I knew I deserved this. And it'll heal."

"And here we are."

After one last look around the full coffee shop, with the clock edging closer to nine, Sarah brought her attention back to the table.

"I need you three to tell the police everything after I'm gone. I need you three to tell the media, talk to the papers, talk to anyone who'll listen after I'm gone."

"Where're you going?" Jessica asked.

"Take out your cell phone and video me entering Adam's art studio on Richmond, then wait outside, videoing the road, the doors."

"Why the road?" Percy asked.

"The second reason I broke your finger, Adam, was because there will be a car accident in about thirty minutes.

The accident involves a volatile propane truck. There will be an explosion. Only one person was supposed to die in that explosion. An artist by the name of Adam DePont. Breaking your finger kept you out of that studio this morning."

Adam blanched, all hostility leaving his pale face.

"Then why are you going in?" Jessica asked, a note of surprise in her tone.

"Because the headline in tomorrow's paper will be about several bodies found in the ensuing fire. Four bodies burned beyond recognition."

Jessica's eyes widened as she figured it out. Percy planted his hands on the table. Adam remained lost in his thoughts.

"You can't tell me you're …" Jessica's voice faded.

"I can, and I am. Film me entering the building. Today, I die in that fire, and the manhunt dies with me. Within thirty minutes, Sarah Roberts ceases to exist, and you three are going to help me kill her."

"I'll help, too," someone said from the table behind her and slightly to the side.

She turned and saw Winters sitting alone, hugging a coffee cup with both palms.

"I had to scope the place out, make sure we were cool," he added. "When I saw you, I wasn't sure why." He turned in his chair to face their table. "But now I know why. I get to be involved in that shit you just said. Now I'm tripping, man."

She slapped him on the shoulder. "Thanks for coming, Winters. But go easy on the enthusiasm."

"Noted."

Sarah finished by telling them the final two things she

needed them to do.

Each agreed to do as she asked.

Without fail.

Chapter 51

Sarah got to the front steps of the Richmond building without seeing Travis Jensen or Joel Blacken. They were either already inside or still scoping out the building.

After one last look over her shoulder, she caught a glimpse of Jessica filming her from across the street. Adam filmed her from behind as he'd followed her to the entrance to his art studio, and Winters stood with Percy, chatting and watching her nonchalantly, making sure they were witnesses as well.

She checked her watch, scanned the street where the accident would occur, and then checked her watch again.

After a moment, her stomach tied up in barbed wire, she entered the building and closed the door behind her. It was the last she would see of them.

Ever.

The common area corridor was empty. She hurried up the steps, walked the old wooden floor as it creaked underfoot to Adam's studio door, and grasped the knob.

After ascertaining she was alone in the hall with a quick look to the left and right, she eased the door open, slipped inside, and closed it quietly behind her.

Outside noise dimmed. A musky odor, like old used wool blankets folded in a closet, wafted up. Her nose twitched with the smell, the urge to sneeze upon her. She squeezed her nose to suppress the urge and lowered to her knees, the door to her back.

Where was everyone? Parkman and Aaron should have been there. Kymberly too.

The room was cavernous, the ceilings at least fifteen feet high. The floor seemed to be made of the same creaky wood as the corridor—each step would announce a person's approach to anyone in earshot. The lights were out, the windows covered, a feeble amount of light creeping in around the shades.

For an art studio, the walls were bare of art. Instead, Adam had only used the studio as a place to work. Several easels of varying sizes stood in disarray throughout the large rectangular room. Stained drop cloths were scattered around as well, and several more were folded and piled six feet high against one wall. Empty frames lined the wall under one of the windows. The rest of the room proved difficult to see with the lights out.

The light was on in the room to her right. The floor creaked from inside that room. Then it creaked again.

Parkman filled the doorway, his shoulders almost touching each side of the doorframe.

"Oh shit," Sarah said. "I didn't know what to expect when I came in. They haven't arrived yet?"

She took a step, then faltered and stopped. Parkman had a large red welt on his cheek. That was new. His eyes seemed bigger like they were bulging. Glazed over, too.

"Sarah," he said, his voice a pitch of fear. "Lock the door."

"Parkman, who's with you?"

"Sarah." He bristled like he wanted to run in fear—or attack someone in anger. "Lock. The. Door."

Sarah waited a moment longer. Without knowing who was there or what the threat was, she had no way of knowing the right plan of action.

The car accident had to be twenty minutes away or less. The four helpers outside would be regrouping, watching their time, preparing to call the police on Sarah. That was one of their final tasks. Call the police a minute before the accident.

Trusting Parkman, she reached back, clasped the thumb latch, and engaged the deadbolt.

Something smashed into Parkman. His head was shoved to the side. He fell out of the doorway, only his feet showing now.

Ready to run, Sarah paused. She had to be careful and survey the threat. She had no intel, and Vivian was quiet again.

Why would her sister send them into these situations and not be there to back them up? How could Vivian think her behavior was acceptable after all the years Parkman had been there with her?

Or maybe this truly was the end.

For all of them.

She stepped forward as Parkman stood up. Sarah crossed the room slowly, listening, but she heard only Parkman getting to his feet. He moved to the side and disappeared beyond view without looking back at her.

One last look at her watch. Twelve minutes to impact. Twelve minutes until the room with the light on, the room where Parkman had just been punched in the face, would be engulfed in flames.

Unless Vivian lied, four people would die in that fire. According to tomorrow's newspaper, that was the story that would run.

I lied, Vivian whispered suddenly in Sarah's head.

Her step faltered at the door.

What?

I lied. Four people will die in eleven minutes, but only two are talked about by the media.

What? Sarah shouted in her head. *Why?*

A man stepped into the open door in front of her. It wasn't his size or height that scared her. It wasn't his bald head, crooked smile, or the thickness of his meaty hands. It was the automatic weapon in his hand, and how he seemed to take great pleasure in aiming it at her.

"Don't shoot her yet," a man said from inside the room. "Bring the meddling bitch to me."

The man stepped out of the lighted room, letting his weapon hang from the strap around his neck, and grabbed her hair. He yanked her down to his waist, pulled, and started back into the room.

Sarah punched at his arm, his abdomen, anything she could hit, but to no avail. The man didn't seem to notice her thrashing.

Instead, he dragged her into the room, then swung his arm as if lobbing a softball underhanded, and let go of her hair. Sarah lost her balance and dropped to the center of the floor.

She pushed the hair out of her eyes and looked around.

Jensen stood with his back to the wall, another beefy man to his left, a thin rope dangling from the man's shoulder. Kymberly kneeled at his feet, bleeding from a split lip.

Behind her, Parkman stood beside Aaron, a black eye already turning an eggplant purple on Parkman's face. Aaron didn't look touched, his face unmarked. But his ragged breathing told her another story; someone had punched him enough times to knock the wind out of him, but he seemed otherwise okay.

It was Blacken who was in mortal danger.

He lay on his side, eyes swollen shut. Blood oozed from his mouth, nose, and left eye. At least two of the fingers on his left hand were broken, bent back, and slightly askew, the index finger taking on a ninety-degree angle at the second knuckle. Something was wrong with his legs, too. Small, white pieces of what looked like spilled gum marked with splotches of red lay scattered around his head. Blacken had a lot of teeth knocked out. Blacken was left untied. Evidently, there was no need.

What the fuck happened here?

"When I got your message," Jensen started, "I sent my

boys here to camp out for the night." He grinned like he was the smartest asshole on the block. He patted the man on the shoulder to his left. "Blacken thought he'd be smart. Show up an hour early, scope out the place." Jensen shook his head, staring at Blacken's unconscious form on the floor. He turned back to Sarah. "Imagine his surprise when my men welcomed him."

Sarah checked the distance to the door, counting the steps to get there. Then, she mentally checked the window distance. The clock on the wall said they had nine minutes left.

"Sarah, before I end all this," he waved an arm at the people assembled about the room like he was a Roman Emperor, "tell me something. How are you involved in my life?"

She gestured at Blacken. "You should have asked him."

"I'm asking you. Why text as if you were Blacken? According to him," Jensen pulled a cell phone out of his back pocket, "and his phone, you sent him a picture of you two," he pointed at Kymberly, "and invited him here. What's your plan? Arrest us? You?"

She glared at Jensen but remained silent.

Eight minutes.

"We're the fucking cops, Sarah. You don't *arrest* us. We arrest you."

"That your plan?" she asked. "Arrest me?"

Jensen eyed her with a look of contempt. He stepped away from the armed men flanking him and stood in front of her. After a moment, he waved for her to stand.

Sarah got to her feet, poised and ready to go for Jensen's

throat, then use him as a shield if his muscle decided to shoot.

"Such a small thing," Jensen said, appraising her. "A small girl with a little mouth. Yet such a large presence with a loud voice. You know, in my day, girls like you were shut down fast."

"We're not in *your* day anymore. This is a new era. Women have a voice." Normally, she wouldn't respond to such bait. She couldn't care less about his opinions or educating him. Stalling him gave her time to think.

"A new era, you say?" He started to walk around her. "Tell me, Sarah, how do you see yourself in this new era? Alive or dead?"

She glanced down to watch his shadow, his feet. She'd duck out of the way if there were a sudden motion of any kind. "I see myself as dead."

"Interesting. I do, too." He stepped around in front of her again. "That's why this place isn't surrounded by cops. That's why, with a manhunt underway for you and me being a sergeant and Blacken a detective, no one is here to arrest you."

"You're going to kill me instead?"

Something moved behind her. Parkman or Aaron. One of the henchmen twitched, his gun rising a notch. The movement ceased.

Jensen barely moved at the provocation.

"Sarah, I'm not going to kill you." His voice took on a drama theater tone like he was playacting. "But I can tell you this: you and your friends won't leave this room alive." He motioned for the man with the rope. "Tie her hands." He pointed at the other man. "Shoot anyone who tries to interfere."

She checked the clock. Something had to be wrong. There was just over four minutes left.

She mumbled it to herself.

"What was that?" Jensen asked. "Repeat yourself."

"None of us will leave here alive in about five minutes."

Jensen looked to his armed men, then back to Sarah. He glanced at Parkman, who shrugged.

"This true?" he asked.

She nodded. "There'll be a car accident outside that window in five minutes. There'll be an explosion. Anyone in this room will be burned alive."

Jensen let a small burst of laughter escape his lips. He held his stomach in an exaggerated expression of how funny he thought her prediction was. His rope man was beside him, untangling it, preparing to tie Sarah.

"No one actually believes you, right?" He looked around the room, stopping on everyone's face. "That you're *psychic*." He shook his head, his shoulders shuddering as if the word deeply offended him. "Whoa, be careful. Sarah's crystal ball holds fateful secrets." He laughed uproariously, his armed men joining in with smiles and subtly hitching their shoulders as well.

The brute took her arm while the other one watched, his gun trained on Aaron and Parkman.

With deft hands, no doubt experienced, the man secured her right hand to a hook in the wall, then set in to work on her left.

She turned enough to catch Aaron's eye. Then glanced

into Parkman's eyes. A knowing glance, an understanding passed between them, and then she turned back to face the armed men.

Her arms were bound to two different hooks, a slight amount of slack in the rope. Sarah stood with her arms outstretched.

Jensen moved to the man on the right. He pointed at Blacken.

The man aimed his weapon. Then fired.

Blacken's body jerked as a bullet entered his forehead above the bridge of his nose. His body shook momentarily in the throes of death as Kymberly knelt close to him, sobbing. She may have hated him enough to leave him, but he was still her husband.

Sarah pulled on her restraints but couldn't go anywhere. Aaron and Parkman were too far away to do anything.

Maybe Jensen would stop at Blacken. Maybe not.

Jensen moved around Sarah, his arms crossed on his chest. He leaned in close and whispered, "You're last. You get to watch everyone else die first." He leaned away, then looked back at Sarah. "People should be made aware of their mistakes by experiencing consequences firsthand."

"Meaning?" she asked.

"Because you invited everyone here, you get to watch them all be shot before you die."

The clock gave them two minutes. Possibly less.

Jensen moved toward the door—toward Parkman and Aaron.

She tensed.

He leaned on the doorframe. One of his armed men

stepped forward, closing the gap on Parkman and Aaron. But that meant he moved within three feet of Sarah.

Jensen raised his hand, held it up momentarily, and then pointed at Parkman.

Virtually beside her, the gunman brought the weapon to bear on Parkman's chest as Aaron jumped in front of Parkman.

Sarah jumped with her one good foot and kicked at the man's knuckles as they whitened with the pressure on the weapon's grip.

She hit the man's hand as the gun fired. Surprised by the impact, the man pulled back reflexively and then pushed toward her. She landed on her foot, then hopped again, thrusting her foot toward his throat. But she missed, her foot bouncing off his thick pectoral muscle.

Then he was on her, shoving her to the floor, his bulk too heavy for her to resist.

"Hold her down," Jensen shouted. "She interferes in everything."

Under the man's weight, she struggled and fought for breath. He'd released his weapon and let it dangle on its cord around his neck like a guitar. Hands free now, he pinned her arms down, his body holding her immobile under him.

When she glanced up, Parkman had blood on his hands.

Parkman. Bleeding.

The sight turned her into a madwoman. She kneed, wrenched, and tried to yank out her arms, but to no avail. The air from her lungs was spent, and she struggled to breathe again.

Out of nowhere, Aaron landed on the man's back. Sarah

hadn't ever seen him fly like his teacher Alex could. The two men scuffled, a mix of flailing arms and legs. It was enough that his weight eased off her, and she gasped in breaths.

The clock said they were out of time. Parkman was on the floor, crawling toward the small doorway that led to the other room. He had a shoulder wound, and it bled profusely, but it didn't appeal fatal.

At any second, the room would ignite and be lost to flames. Where was Jensen? Kymberly?

The second gunman appeared above her and dove on Aaron. Kymberly ran by on Sarah's right. The men fought, grunts and groans, fists landing. Someone was bleeding.

Jensen shouted something. The room had dropped into chaos.

Sarah pulled on her restraints.

A gun fired.

Kymberly dropped from sight.

Jensen had shot his mistress. This was all wrong. It was going to hell, and they would all die.

Above her, Aaron lost his grip on one of the men. The other man elbowed Aaron in the cheek. His eyes rolled back in his head, and he dropped beside Sarah.

She screamed.

Both of Jensen's men lay on top of Sarah and Aaron.

There was no way out for either of them. They would burn alive and die in seconds.

Parkman had been the only one who made it to the door, but would he get out the barn doors on the side of the building in time?

Jensen stepped over the top of her, gun in hand.

"Start praying, Sarah," Jensen said. "If you're the religious type."

He walked around so he wasn't upside down to her, his man lying on her as if they were having sex in the missionary position. He even pushed with his pelvic area, adding pressure to her crotch.

Jensen placed the weapon at her throat as his man eased down her body, still keeping her forced down with his hands as they toured her sides, then her thighs.

She stared up at Jensen, a maniacal look in his eyes. He was going to do it. He was going to pull the trigger while his hired thug kept his weight on her thighs.

Then the building shook.

Jensen looked behind him. His mouth opened in a silent scream as the window broke inward. Something clicked outside. Someone screamed. The room lit up as flames covered the area in seconds.

Sarah flattened herself on the floor, covering her face. The man on her thighs dropped, all his weight pushing her knees backward into the floor.

Jensen dropped onto her upper body.

A wave of heat washed over her, searing all the hair on her forearms. Then, her hands were free of the small rope, and she drew them under Jensen's body.

Several moments later, the initial blast over, the walls and parts of the floor aflame, she glanced over at Aaron. He was awake and untouched by flame but missing his eyebrows and lashes. The back of the man on top of him was on fire.

Aaron shoved the man to the side, coughed, and rolled toward her. He was able to shove Jensen off and kicked at the man on her legs.

Her hands ached from the initial blast, but she was fine, minus a little singed hair.

Jensen and his two men were unconscious, knocked out by the blast that they had somehow shielded her and Aaron from. Blacken was dead. That was the four bodies in the room, just as Vivian had said. The flames grew more intense as she rolled toward the door Parkman and Kymberly had gone through.

Sarah took one last look into the room that held Blacken's body, Jensen, and his two henchmen.

Then another explosion leveled the wall between the two rooms and knocked Sarah out, the heat searing her flesh.

Chapter 52

LACEE FAUST WIPED THE last of the tables, dropped her apron in the laundry bin, and headed to the back room to punch out.

Throughout her morning shift, several customers leaving the motel spoke of the accident and fire downtown near Spadina Avenue in the fashion district. Some warned of the roads being cut off, and others of the tourist sites that would be missed that day.

Through their combined dismay—and perhaps a little sorrow for the lives lost—Lacee had snuck a look at her phone on her fifteen-minute break for an update.

CP24 had reported the accident involved three vehicles, one a truck carrying propane. A corner unit of a building on Richmond Street had been instantly engulfed in flames. Witnesses in the area were interviewed. A man named Adam

DePont claimed to be using the damaged space as an art studio.

Lacee watched a live version of the interview and listened while Adam spoke about having broken his finger recently. If he hadn't broken it, he would've been inside his studio at the time of the accident. His broken finger saved his life.

Someone else said he saw the fugitive Sarah Roberts enter the art studio. He claimed to have it on camera and would sell it to CP24. A woman named Jessica Russell confirmed that Sarah Roberts was in the studio when it went up in flames. She had called in a tip to the OPP mere seconds before the accident happened, as every police agency in the country was still looking for Sarah.

"It appears Sarah Roberts may have met a bitter end," the CP24 anchor said. "Reports are coming in that several bodies are still inside the studio. This is a multiple-casualty situation at Richmond and Spadina."

After listening to a report at the hospital, which talked about Parkman and Kymberly Blacken being admitted, Lacee shut off her phone and got back to work.

Now she grabbed her keys, exited the back door of the café, and jogged to her minivan. It was already gassed up and loaded with enough food for two days' travel. Once on the highway headed into downtown Toronto, she turned on the radio and listened to Honeymoon Suite sing about a "New Girl Now." Her speakers vibrated in the dash as she took the Spadina Avenue exit and headed north. Up ahead, police officers guided traffic around the Richmond Street intersection. Three blocks short of Richmond, Lacee took a right onto Front Street, then an immediate left onto Blue Jays Way. One more quick left, and she was on Wellington, headed toward the Clarence Square Dog Park, where Sarah told her to meet them.

She eased onto the curb by a small copse of trees where two people sat on a park bench, clicked to unlock the doors, and waited.

She didn't have to wait long.

The side door opened, and two people hopped in, slamming the door shut quickly. Without a word, they settled in the back and covered up with the king-sized blanket Lacee had supplied.

She hit the gas. At Spadina, she turned left and headed back toward the Gardiner Expressway. Once on the elevated highway, she sped toward the Queen Elizabeth Way, ensuring to stay at the speed of traffic.

She checked her mirror periodically to catch a glimpse of her passengers. She couldn't see them in her minivan's dark, windowless rear.

On Highway 403, headed toward Hamilton, she couldn't wait any longer.

"You guys okay?" she asked after another glance in the mirror.

Aaron lifted his head. "Yeah. Just exhausted." He cleared his throat. "Any word on Parkman? We saw them take him by ambulance."

Lacee nodded. "Around eleven this morning, it was reported he was in surgery but going to be fine. Kymberly too. He's under heavy guard at the hospital."

Sarah lifted her head from under the blanket. "Casper'll

be there to help. Parkman's done nothing wrong."

Lacee was overwhelmed with emotion. "It's so good to see you both. I was worried."

"Worried?"

"That I'd drive up to the dog park, and no one would come. The news this morning—" Emotion choked off her words.

"The news?" Aaron asked. "This morning?"

Lacee swallowed, cleared her throat, and stared at the road. "The news said there were multiple casualties at the site. They speculated that perhaps Sarah Roberts had died in the fire. Several witnesses claim you entered the art studio but weren't seen leaving."

Lacee watched in the mirror as Sarah rested back on her elbow.

"Everyone's doing as they're supposed to." Sarah coughed.

"Meaning?" Lacee asked.

"As far as the world's concerned, Sarah Roberts is dead."

"And that's a good thing?" Her voice rose a notch. "We need you, Sarah."

"Not right now. Aaron needs me. I need me."

"Are you finished with automatic writing, listening to your sister? Finished for good?"

"It's been a long time since I started. Many years of helping others. I've been through a lot." She lowered her head to look at her lap. "I can't say I'm finished for good. I'm sure something'll come up one day. But I can say I'm finished for a while."

"What's a while? A couple of months? Couple of years?

Decades?"

Sarah shrugged. "Not sure. It could be months, years, or decades. Maybe I'll never go back." She nestled closer to Aaron, then coughed again. "Maybe we'll start a family. We'll be free once Darwin and his wife secure us new names and passports. Sarah Roberts will stay dead forever."

"Is that what you want?" Lacee asked. "Forever?" Lacee drove on in silence, watching the road ahead, wondering if they heard her question.

Then Sarah said, "No. I want to help people. I love what I do. But it has to be on my terms, my way. It's too reckless to be drawn into the machinations of others and their plans. Being betrayed by cops, framed for murder by cops, and ultimately *killed* by cops, I can say my distrust for them has gone back to square one. I need out of this life for a while. I need a vacation. Been wanting one for too many years, and now Vivian promised me one."

"I sure hate to see you go," Lacee said. "But after all you've done, I understand. And I'm honored to be the one to take you across the border. I've never done anything as illegal as smuggling someone into the States."

"I'm American," Sarah said. "You're really only smuggling Aaron, my Canadian boyfriend, across."

"Once we're in the States, have you considered where you want to go?"

"We were thinking of heading to the coast, finding a small town, and setting up house."

"The coast? Like the Atlantic coast?"

"No, the Pacific. We even picked a state."

"Which one?"

"Oregon."

Lacee changed lanes as they passed Stoney Creek on the other side of Hamilton.

"Portland?" Lacee asked.

"We were thinking something smaller in that area. But who knows? We'll drive across the States and see where we end up."

It was Lacee's turn to shrug. "Sounds good to me."

"Lacee, we really appreciate all you're doing for us. Will your son be okay?"

"I'm only gone overnight. Mom's got him."

"And you'll wait five or six days before you report this minivan as stolen?"

"I'll wait longer if you need it."

"We don't know how to thank you, Lacee."

"There is one way."

Sarah and Aaron glanced at each other in her mirror.

"Promise me you'll think about coming back one day, even if it's a year or two from now. Just say you'll think about it. That'll be good enough for me."

"I can do that. I promise."

"I can see it now," Aaron said. "The headline will read, *Sarah's Return* or something like that."

"If it's too soon, it'll say, *Sarah's Arrest.*"

They drove in silence until they reached the border crossing. Lacee played her part expertly, and soon, she was driving the minivan in Niagara Falls, New York.

After ten minutes, she pulled over and offered Aaron the keys.

They hugged on the side of the road with promises to

keep in touch, both parties knowing that wouldn't work.

"Stay safe, Sarah," Lacee said. "Take care of her, Aaron."

Lacee watched her minivan drive off toward the main interstate and wiped a tear from her eye.

Sarah Roberts was gone with no idea where she was going or if she would ever return to help anyone again.

Sarah Roberts was gone.

Lacee turned and started toward the bus depot, hoping to hear the name Sarah Roberts again one day.

If not, she sure had a hell of a story to tell her son when he was older.

One hell of a story …

"Goodbye, Sarah." She stopped and looked over her shoulder. The van was gone from sight. "Goodbye."

Lacee walked away, tears slipping from her eyes.

Afterword

DEAR READER,

Thank you for coming on this journey with me. It's been one hell of a ride.

Sarah has been a large part of my life and always will be for some time. I wrote *Dark Visions* in 2002 and wondered in those early days if I would write a sequel. When I decided to in 2010, I wrote *The Warning*. Then, I immediately decided to make it a trilogy and wrote *The Crypt*. At the end of *The Crypt*, when Sarah got to Armond Stuart, I was done with the Sarah Roberts Series. After great reviews, letters, and messages from readers, I could see Sarah was loved, and more novels were needed. So, I started on book four and on and on, thinking I'd get to seven or possibly ten books one day.

By the time I got to ten Sarah books, I had thought I'd never stop. And you know what, I still don't think I'll stop. *Sarah's Return*, book twenty-one, was released in 2020, and man, what a book that one was. All the past characters are involved in *Sarah's Return* because unknown forces try to stop her when she returns to deal with a human procurement company. *Sarah's Return* is vicious and unrelenting.

I will say this: the series is far from over.

There's much more to come. But in the meantime, I have more standalone novels coming, too.

With book twenty, I wanted to harken back to Sarah's past. *Dark Visions* started this series around Sarah's lack of trust for cops—she hated cops in the early books. Bring in Parkman in book two, a cop who loves Sarah, and we see her softening her dislike for them throughout the series.

But in book twenty, *The Betrayal*, it was the cops who betrayed her. The police, for their selfish motivations, wanted Sarah off the streets. A subtle nod to book nineteen with the Lombardi connection and Blacken's access to Sarah's cell number and whereabouts gave me the idea. I thought Joel Blacken was a dirtbag with an agenda. He wanted someone to kill his wife so she couldn't take half *his* stuff when she *left* him. He also orchestrated Russell's attack on the bus and whispered in the right ears that Sarah was to be blamed. Set up Jensen's men with the bad information on the gang attack at the motel, and you have a stage set for Sarah to come in and try to stay alive while saving others.

I pulled from a true story for those interested in where some of these ideas and locations come from. The scene when Russell meets up with Parkman and tells him that he's despondent at what he has done, that there's no way out for him—that's a true story.

Let me explain …

For research for the novel *The Drowning*, I took on a job locally as a security officer. I committed to the security company for at least three months, but I chose to do five months. They hired me on as a mobile patrol officer. I had a specific geographical area where I drove during twelve-hour shifts, checking sites and watching for vagrants, damage, and unlocked doors.

One night, during my rounds at a local church where I would walk the perimeter, I hopped back into my security cruiser and noticed a pickup truck, a man sitting in it alone in the back parking area. Since this area was private property after ten in the evening, I drove over and rolled down my window. The driver of the pickup did the same.

We chatted.

It was pretty close to what happened in this novel between Russell and Parkman, except for the warning to Sarah and the Blacken information. The driver told me he had done things he couldn't come back from. Bus and train stations were being watched. His family was threatened. He was sad, morose, and despondent. He oozed a sense akin to giving up—it would be better if he were dead, for him and his family—the edge of suicide around the corner as that would solve everything. The man wore Kevlar and said he didn't think he would make the week.

Hells Angels have a large presence in this city. I understood from him that he had wronged them in some way.

Then he hit the gas and drove off.

After talking to that man, it left me with a feeling of utter hopelessness. He had spoken about himself as if it was all over like there was no point in moving forward because nothing ahead would be pleasant.

I wanted to capture a little of that for Russell. Russell's gambling debts caused him to sabotage the brakes on the prison bus. It was too much to handle when he discovered he had killed his brother. He wouldn't complete his task to arrest Parkman on a trumped-up charge. Instead, he offered the warning. Then he went after Blacken and almost got him.

Now, onto our guests …

I want to thank Echo Bos, Teresa Wiitanen, Janet Kirsten, Debbie Clanton, Bethany Carpenter, and Lacee Faust for allowing me to use their names as characters in this book.

Also, a special thank you goes out to Cleta Mathis for giving me the title of this novel almost two years before it was written.

That said, I want to end on a special note.

Lacee Faust reached out many years ago as a reader of the Sarah Roberts Series and told me she had spoken to her sister and mother about the series. Lacee's family then went on to read the series, and I've been blessed and honored to be in touch with all of them over the years.

When Lacee read *Dark Visions* back in 2011, something clicked for her. It uniquely connected with Lacee, and Sarah moved her in ways that filled my heart.

Then I received a letter from Lacee. It was addressed to Sarah Roberts. After that, I received a poem from Lacee.

The poem made me cry.

Lacee Faust, you inspire me to write Sarah Roberts novels until I physically can't anymore. You remind me of my responsibility to the reader and how important the reader/writer relationship is. Because of you, Lacee, and the story that you so bravely offer below, I applaud you.

If anyone out there is currently experiencing or dealing with anything remotely close to what you're about to read, please, I beg you, reach out to someone. There is hope. There is life on the other side of pain. Make a choice. Make a decision.

You're worth it.

Now, I turn the rest of the Afterword over to Lacee Faust.

I dedicate this novel to anyone—male or female—being abused, held down, or controlled in any way. Get out from under and stand tall. Love yourself more than they proclaim to love you because they likely don't.

We support you.

Jonas Saul

(Lacee Faust's words are below)

Dear Sarah Roberts,

In 2011, I purchased a book called *Dark Visions*. I met you on page one. Before I could even turn the first page, it was obvious that you were battling some sort of internal demon. Something troubled you, and at that moment, I wanted to reach out and help in any way I could—the way I wished someone would've helped me when I needed it had I asked them to.

At that time in my life, I had just broken the chain that linked me to an abusive man. He was killing my spirit little by little as each day I let it go on. My abuse was something I kept quiet from everyone, and until now, I've only allowed a small number of people to know the demons I have buried inside me from that time in my life.

You received visits from your dead sister, which comforted me, as I had never met someone who had a similar experience as myself.

Before I was born, my maternal grandfather passed on. I never got to meet him, nor even look at him, except in photographs.

But that soon changed.

My older sister and I shared a room when we were young. I had woken in the middle of the night once to my grandfather standing in the corner of my room, staring at me. He didn't speak, but somehow, I knew it was him. He smiled, and then I drifted back to sleep. Upon waking the next morning, I assumed it was all a dream, but then my sister asked me something that startled me.

"Did you see Grandpa last night?" she asked.

I thought she knew about my dream for a brief moment but soon concluded that it was no dream. What I had experienced was real and something pretty special. I've been a believer in the other side since.

Sarah, so many things you said throughout your story brought me hope. Hope for a brighter future. Hope for strength and determination. Hope for confidence in myself, to know I could break through any obstacles in my way, and to never lessen who I was by the hands of someone else.

When you were being held captive inside the trunk of a car, you yelled out, "Help!" I envied your strength at that moment. As simple as it was, that four-letter word was something I had been too weak to ask. I knew it would bring questions I wasn't ready to answer, so I kept quiet ... until later.

In chapter 27, you were asked, "What happened to your hair?" Your response was just as comical as it was powerful. You replied, "It's a disease. It's contagious." Regardless of the tribulations you were experiencing, you had not let go of your sense of humor, and your determination to survive would not let him "break you." You would not let him know the fear you held inside. Through my pain, I had lost my sense of being and my sense of humor. I had stopped seeing the good in others for a while. This moment was important, and my eyes were wide open.

Once you escaped, you put your concern for others above yours. In chapter 50, speaking to a stranger, you said, "He kidnapped me a few days ago. Please, just get me to a phone, then leave." This amazed me. I was petrified for you and was afraid of you being alone. I could not fathom the determination you had to survive. Putting your concern for this stranger above your own was quite moving for me.

Finally, toward the end of the book, you said to Alex, "I'm okay. Don't take me to a hospital just yet. Not until we catch up with the asshole that snatched me." You had survived. You were tough and held the power to move forward. Yet you wanted revenge, you wanted answers, and you wanted the perpetrator to have consequences. As a woman who had once been held captive at the hands of her abuser, you made me feel empowered again. A feeling that all of us who have experienced such things have wanted as well. My abuser never suffered, and he was never dealt consequences, but somehow, through you, I would get my revenge.

Below is a poem I wrote, inspired by you, Sarah, and dedicated to anyone out there, male or female, living under hostile conditions.

I once felt secure when you held me so close.
But months later, that changed when an argument arose.
I said I was sorry when I had done nothing wrong.
I tried to make peace so the pain wouldn't be prolonged.

I knew what was coming as you occluded my cries.
When I begged you to stop, with tears in my eyes.
You struck me the first time, over the dinner I burned.
It was my fault I was bleeding that night, I soon learned.

You told me "to be quiet," but me, you ought not to blame.
You justified your actions through your guilt and your shame.
The next morning, you were sorry, with roses and daisies.
What you had done to me no longer dismayed me.

The beatings progressed, but reluctantly, I stayed.
Your soft words spoken were well-versed and played.
Your manipulation was obvious to everyone but me.
Your control was strong, yet I was too ignorant to see.

My face burned like fire after being backhanded.
So I distanced my friends, as you had demanded.
Ice was dumped in my face one night as I slept.
You smiled and laughed, and you watched while I wept.

My feet were pulled from beneath me when I ran to get away.
You stole my self-worth from me, so I chose to stay.
You used my son as a bargaining chip when I begged to let us leave.
I had to do what pleased you before you'd give him back to me.

You threw house keys at me, but they fell on my son.
He jerked in his sleep, and you smiled at what you'd done.
You held me down after on that cold, grimy floor.
You slapped my face and my clothes you tore.

I held back my cries so my son would rest; I refused to let him see.
You pulled my hair, squeezed my breasts, and then raped me.
You told me you loved me and that I was warm and tight.
I envisioned leaving you for good later that same night.

I lay there while you finished, as that would be your last.
The bruises were all over me, but they would be in my past.
The abuse would be over when I walked through that door.
When we went outside after, you called me a whore.

The door slammed behind us as I left you for good.
Through the window, you smiled, and I knew where I stood.
I was no longer fearful of you, which damaged your pride.
Then I left you behind, with my son at my side.

I was no longer blinded to who I had become.
A girl who had allowed her heart to go numb.
Thank you for gifting me the lesson that day.
I then felt empowered, and still, here I stay.

Thank you, Lacee Faust. Thank you for your strength, your honesty, and your bravery. If anyone wants to reach out to Lacee for any reason, she has authorized me to offer her direct email.
You can reach Lacee at laceefaust (at) gmail (dot) com.

Sarah Roberts will live on …
See you all again.
Very soon.
Jonas Saul

About Jonas Saul

Jonas Saul is the bestselling author of the Sarah Roberts
Series—more than two million sold!—and has written
and published over sixty thrillers. After acquiring an
agent, he signed several deals in Los Angeles, with
MadRiver Pictures optioning his Sarah Roberts Series—
over forty books!—(currently in development).

Jonas has often outranked Stephen King and Dean

Koontz on Amazon over the past decade. He's regularly invited to be a guest speaker, teacher, or workshop presenter at international writing conferences and film festivals worldwide. He hosts an annual writer's retreat in Greece, where he currently lives. He focuses his teaching on how to get tension and emotion in every scene, on every page, how he made it as a creator/writer, the path to success in this business, and the pitfalls to avoid. He also hosts a reading retreat in Greece with guest authors, yoga retreats, and hiking retreats. Visit the Imagine Greece Retreats website at www.imaginegreeceretreats.com, or email him directly to discuss an opportunity to join one of the retreats here: jonas@imaginegreeceretreats.com.

Jonas is also a professional freelance editor. He works for several publishers and does private editing for clients, with many testimonials on his website at www.imaginepress.org, which details each author's response to Jonas's editing skills. Email Jonas directly for an editing quote here: editor@imaginepress.org.

To book Jonas for a speaking engagement at a writer's conference/festival, to have him on your jury at a film festival, or even to say hello, email Jonas directly at jonas@icloud.com.

For updates on releases, hit the "Follow" button on Amazon or Bookbub, and join Jonas on Facebook, where he's most active.

Contact Jonas Saul

Linktree: Find me here

www.ingramcontent.com/pod-product-compliance
Lightning Source LLC
Chambersburg PA
CBHW022013310726
48972CB00006B/1638